Henry and Friends

These stories are dedicated to my beloved
granddaughters,Isabella and Francesca,
for whom they were first told

Contents

Published by Northwood Publishing

Copyright © 2009, 2020 Cynthia Harrod-Eagles

All rights reserved

ISBN 978-1-84396-606-7

Illustrations copyright © 2009 Ann Kronheimer

Pre-press production
eBook Versions
27 Old Gloucester Street
London WC1N 3AX
www.ebookversions.com

Henry and the Big, Wide World

Once upon a time there was a paper bag named Henry. He was a most splendid bag, with handsome stripes of dark blue and a sharply deckled edge that he was very proud of. He lived under the counter in a bookshop in Northwood, in a pile with all his brothers and sisters. They all looked just like him, but even so, Henry was sure he must be a little bit handsomer and cleverer than them, in some way.

Life was rather dull under the counter, for there wasn't much to see, and nothing at all to do. But every paper bag knew that one day he would reach the top of the pile, and then his real life would begin. On that day, the hand of the shopkeeper would come down and whisk him away, out into the big, wide world. Then *really* exciting things would start to happen.

The paper bags talked together all the time about what it might be like out there, but since none of them ever came back to tell the story, they really had no idea what happened afterwards. They only knew the adventure waiting for them would be wonderful. It was, they were sure, what they had all been created for. Though paper bags are quiet fellows on the whole, they have bold spirits and long for excitement.

Meanwhile they passed the time by watching the customers come and go. When each person came into the shop, they liked to guess what sort of book they would buy. Would it be a love story, or a crime story, or one about war and battles and guns? Sometimes they would have a competition, and Henry often won. He was good at guessing. As he got near the top of the pile, the other bags admired and respected him more, and he was almost sorry that one day he would have to leave them. But he could hardly wait for that day to come and his adventure to begin.

At last came the day and came the hour when Henry was at the top of the pile. It had been a busy day, and his brothers and sisters had been departing one after the other all morning.

'I shall be off soon,' he whispered to the bags below him. 'I shall be off to see the big, wide world!' He watched the customers coming in through the door, and browsing among the books. Which of them would it be? The young man with the rucksack, who might be a student, and was reading a history book? The young woman in the short skirt browsing through the romances? The tall man in spectacles who was looking at a book about a famous politician?

'Have a guess, Henry!' the other bags urged him. 'Guess which one's yours.'

But Henry was too nervous to guess. His whole life was about to change, and the way it changed would depend on which person took him. It was too important to make a game of. He could only wait and see what happened. He had been under the counter since the day he came from the factory, and he knew nothing about the world outside.

Then at last the shopkeeper reached for him.

'This is it! I'm off!' he shouted in great excitement. 'Goodbye, everyone!'

'Goodbye Henry!' the other bags said. 'Good luck! Good luck!'

'Come back one day and tell us all about it!' they cried.

'I'll try,' he said. 'Goodbye!'

He was plucked out into the light, placed on top of the counter, and now he could see everything. How big the shop seemed, now he could see it properly! And here was his customer – his very own, sent for him alone. It was a nice old lady, who had come into the shop to buy a storybook for her little granddaughters. Henry had been chosen to hold the book.

'What a nice bag,' the Granny said as she set eyes on Henry.

Henry swelled with pride. No human had ever said anything nice about him before, and he found he liked the sensation very much.

'Don't you worry,' he whispered to the book as it was slipped inside him. 'I'll take good care of you, and keep you nice and clean.'

The book did not answer – for you see, it was not a *talking* book.

7

The Granny paid the shopkeeper, and then took up Henry with the book inside him, and went out of the shop.

Down the street she walked with Henry in her hand. He gazed about him in astonishment. *I'm outside*, he thought. *Oh, look at the world, how large it is*! He stared in wonder at all the cars and vans and bicycles rushing past in the road. How noisy it was after the quiet of the bookshop! He marvelled at all the people walking by, some this way and some that, women with pushchairs and shopping bags, men with their hands in their pockets, children of all sizes, dogs on leads. He had not thought there could be so many people in the world. How much movement there was, after the stillness under the counter!

He looked at the shops, so full of things to buy, and he felt a burst of pride, knowing that inside each shop there would be paper bags like him, ready to do their duty. The world could not get by without paper bags, and that was a fact! Humans needed them, depended on them. It made him feel very important. He wanted to shout out, 'Look at me, everyone! I'm Henry, and I'm a paper bag! I'm taking care of this book for my human!' But he didn't – mostly because he was too excited, and too busy looking around.

At last the Granny reached her car, which was standing in the car park at the bottom of the street. She got in and put Henry on the front seat beside her, and drove away. It was a long drive, but Henry didn't mind, because there was so much to see. So this was the big, wide world! He gazed at the tops of the buildings rushing by, at the tops of trees. He could see the sky, so blue, and with billows of white cloud in it, and thought how much prettier it was than the underside of the counter, which had been the only sky he had known for the whole of his life until now.

After a while they left the town, and there were fields, some with grass and some with crops growing in them; some with animals in them and some empty. There were hills reaching up into the sky, with trees covering them like dark green fur. He saw tall pylons, like the skeletons of giants, marching away over the countryside to the horizon. There were birds flying by overhead, and all the time sky, and more sky.

Why, he thought, *the world isn't big, it's enormous!* And he felt just a little nervous, and almost wished himself safely back in his stuffy home under the shop counter. But his excitement was greater than his fear. He was starting on the great adventure of life, and he wanted very badly to know what would happen next.

At last the Granny reached the cottage out in the country where her grandchildren lived. She parked the car and carried Henry up to the door, and rang the bell. A tall lady opened it – she was the Granny's daughter, and the mother of the grandchildren. And behind her Henry could see the granddaughters – two little fair-haired girls who looked exactly alike. Henry himself had had lots of brothers and sisters who looked exactly like him. He was most interested to find that human beings could be twins, just like paper bags!

How sweet they looked, Henry thought, *how pretty!* He felt proud that he had brought them a book, and kept it clean and nice for them. How they would love him and admire him! They would treasure him for ever. So this, then, would be his new life – to take care of the book for his two little angels.

Now the Granny gave Henry to the little girls. 'Here's something for you, my dears,' she said.

'Oh, thank you, Granny!' cried Betty, the first little girl.

'We love books!' said Polly, the other one.

Henry was pleased that they loved books. It would make them value him even more. Their little hands were gripping him tightly, and they tugged him about, each one wanting to be the one to hold him. *Goodness, they're fighting over me!* Henry thought. *If only the others could see me now. How lucky I am! I must be the happiest paper bag in the world!*

But then something dreadful happened. Betty had hold of him, and Polly had hold of the book. They tugged in opposite directions, and the book came out. There was nothing Henry could do about it.

He shouted, 'Look out!' but no one heard him. Oh dear, oh dear! Now the book would get dirty, without him to take care of it.

'Put it back!' he cried, but no one heard him.

Then something worse happened. The little girl who was holding him threw him down on the floor.

'Hey!' shouted Henry. 'You've dropped me! Hey, I'm down here!'

She took not the slightest notice, and nor did her sister. They were both holding the book, opening the pages, exclaiming over the pictures.

'Oh, Granny, it's lovely! Will you read it to us?' they cried.

They took the Granny's hand and pulled her to the sofa to sit down. And one! Two! Three! Four! Their little feet trampled over Henry as he lay forgotten on the floor.

Henry lay there, stunned. He couldn't understand what was happening. Why hadn't they picked him up again? They were sitting now with the Granny, one either side of her, and all three were gazing at the book as if it were the most interesting thing in the world. They didn't seem to understand that Henry was lying there so close to them. Wasn't he more important than the book? But they weren't paying him any attention.

And then Henry understood, and his heart broke. They didn't care about him. They didn't love him. He had brought them the book in perfect condition, but they weren't grateful to him. They had thrown him away, and now they had forgotten him. It was as if he didn't exist any more.

So this was his wonderful adventure, he thought bitterly. It was all over already! He had gone out into the big, wide world to find a new life, and now it seemed that the new life had ended almost before it had begun. He was despised and discarded. What would happen to him next? Would it be the rubbish bin for him? He had heard terrible stories of bins and rubbish sacks and something awful called a landfill site. He had hoped never to know about them at first hand. And then there was something bags didn't even like to talk about, something called *recycling* . . . If paper bags could cry, Henry would have wept hot tears of self-pity. He couldn't bear to think that there was nothing more for him to look forward to.

This was the worst moment of his life, and he wished with all his heart that he had never left the bookshop. No, he wished he had never left the factory!

But then, just as Henry thought no paper bag had ever been more miserable, something wonderful happened.

The Mother, who had been watching the scene with a pleased smile, saw Henry. She made a tutting noise and said, 'Don't leave that bag lying on the floor, girls. How many times do I have to tell you?'

11

She reached down and picked Henry up. She smoothed him between her fingers – oh, how good that felt to Henry, who had always been proud of his crisp newness and his fine stripes! The Mother was looking at him with interest and approval.

'This is a really nice bag,' she said. 'Much too nice to throw away. I shall keep it. It's sure to come in useful some time.'

Henry was lifted up from despair into new hope. Someone did value him! Someone admired him! Perhaps his new life was not over after all!

'Would you like a cup of tea, Mum?' the Mother asked the Granny.

'Yes please, dear,' said the Granny.

'I'll put the kettle on, then,' said the Mother, and she went into the kitchen, still carefully carrying Henry. In the kitchen there was a great Welsh dresser made of old pine wood. It had long shelves above, covered in plates patterned with blue and white hoops. Henry noted them with pleasure because they were rather like his own stripes. There were striped mugs hanging on hooks under the shelves. And there were three cupboards below, with three drawers above them. The Mother opened one of the drawers, and Henry saw it was full of other paper bags, all different shapes and sizes and colours, together with pieces of string and rubber bands and useful things like that.

'I'll put you in here,' said the Mother, and laid Henry gently on the top of the pile, and then shut the drawer.

It was dark in there, and quiet, and pleasantly stuffy, rather like his old home, which made it feel nice and safe. There was nothing to see, of course, and for the moment nothing at all to do, but Henry didn't mind. He was sure his life was not over, now that he knew the Mother admired and valued him. One day the drawer would open, and he would be whisked away into the big, wide world for another adventure. Meanwhile, he was content to rest in safety in this cosy drawer.

The other paper bags made him welcome, asked his name and where he had come from. Henry was happy to pass the time telling them all about his adventures so far. They were so eager to hear him that perhaps we can forgive him if he embroidered a little to make them sound more exciting than they were. After all, days in the drawer could seem rather long, and there was nothing to do in there but tell stories!

Henry's Ride Home

The days were long in the dresser drawer, and all much the same. Henry had told his story so often, and in so many different ways, that he was good and ready for another adventure by the time the drawer opened again. The Mother had come looking for a paper bag.

All the bags began rustling excitedly when her hand came down among them. 'Take me! Take me!' they whispered, trying to push themselves forward. But it was Henry she wanted.

'That's not fair!' the other bags cried as he soared away. 'We were here first.'

'Sorry, you lot!' he called down to them. 'It's just the luck of the drawer!'

The Mother smoothed Henry in her hands in the way he liked. 'You'll do. Just the right size,' she said. She was smiling, and Henry was certain the smile was for him. She really, really loved him, he thought.

The Mother was taking some papers to do with Betty's and Polly's

14

school, to show them to a friend. She put the papers into Henry and tucked him under her arm, and soon enough they were off.

It was exciting to be out of doors again, and Henry had a good look round on the way to the car, so that he could tell the others everything when he got back. The cottage they lived in, he found, sat beside the road at a high point of a great heath. The land was studded with scrub and bushes and clumps of trees, and rolled away on all sides, down towards a misty blue-grey streak that Henry thought might be the sea. He looked back at the cottage. It was square and neat and pretty, with green shutters and a creeper scrambling over it, and there was a sign on the gate that said *Honeysuckle Cottage*. Henry took special note of that. He wondered if any of the chaps in the drawer knew the name of the place they lived. He bet they didn't! He'd enjoy telling them that.

The car drive was not so interesting, because Henry was on the floor and all he could see was the sky. There was an awful lot of *that*, however, and he began to fancy himself something of an expert on the different kinds of cloud there were in it. At last they arrived at the friend's house. It did not stand all alone like his home, but was part of a row of houses all joined together, facing an open field on the other side of the road.

The Mother took him in, was greeted by her friend, and then the papers were taken out of Henry and the two women carried them away to look at them together. Henry was left empty, lying on a table beside the half-open window.

Henry had a good look round the room, but it was quite small and he had soon memorised everything in it. He was just beginning to feel a little bored when a butterfly came in at the window.

'Hello!' said Henry. 'What's your name?'

The Butterfly gave him a look of great surprise, and flew down and landed on him. It was very light, and its feet tickled him. It walked round in a circle, touching Henry with its feelers, and muttered, 'A talking bag! Whatever next?' Then it sat still, opened and closed its wings a few times, and cleaned its face carefully. 'Nice and warm to sit on, however,' the Butterfly said to itself. 'Quite pleasant for the time of year.'

It still didn't answer Henry's question, even when Henry repeated it. 'Why won't you talk to me?' he asked.

'Busy, busy, busy!' the Butterfly cried in its fluttery little voice. 'So busy.'

'Oh, not too busy to talk, surely? Stay for a while and tell me your story.'

'Can't *stay*,' said the Butterfly in a shocked voice. 'Things to do. Places to be. Mustn't stop, you know. No time to sit still.' It fluttered up on to some flowers in a vase on the same table. It inserted its long tongue into each flower in turn, murmuring, 'Oh dear, oh dear! Nothing here for me. Nothing at all. What a life! Must move on. Mustn't linger. Places to see, things to visit.' And it fluttered up towards the window.

'Oh, please stay!' Henry called.

But the Butterfly paid him no attention. It fluttered out into the sunshine and away, still murmuring, 'Busy, busy, busy.'

Well, thought Henry, *he wasn't much company!* And he began to feel very bored, and wished something else would happen.

Something else did. A fly came in through the open half of the window and landed on Henry. It was rather beautiful, with a shiny green-and-gold back, delicate wings and a handsome red face. It was even lighter than the butterfly, and as it walked round in circles on its tiny hairy feet, touching Henry curiously with its long snout and tongue, it tickled so much that Henry couldn't help laughing.

'Woah!' the Fly shouted, flying up in the air in alarm. 'Earthquake! Earthquake!'

'It's all right,' said Henry. 'It's only me. I won't hurt you.'

'Help! Help! A talking bag!' the Fly yelled, dashing back and forth in the air above him in a complete panic. 'Monsters! Assassins!'

'Don't be afraid. Why are you so timid?' Henry called. 'I'd like to be your friend.'

'Friend? I don't have any friends. Everyone hates me. Everyone keeps trying to kill me.'

'Well, I don't want to kill you. I just want to talk to you. Come and sit down.'

'Oh, I know that trick,' said the Fly bitterly. 'I sit down and then – wham! I've been walloped by your sort before now. All sorts of paper. Folded up for the purpose. All innocent and nice as you please, and then – wallop! Well, I'm not falling for it again. I'm off!' It flew fast towards the window. But it missed the opening and banged into the glass of the closed part. At once it became hysterical. 'The air's turned solid! It's black magic! Sorcery! I'm doomed!' it shouted. It hurled itself at the window over and over again, banging its head into the glass every time and yelling, 'Help! Demons! Monsters! Help! Help!'

Henry was exasperated. The bottom half of the window was wide open, and just as big as the top half. Why couldn't the Fly find it?

'You keep missing the opening!' he shouted at the Fly. 'Just go a bit lower and you'll get out!'

The fly was in too much of a panic to listen. Bang, bang, bang against the glass it went. But at last, by sheer chance, it threw itself at the open half of the window and hurtled out to freedom.

At once its panic disappeared. It flew round a few times then landed on the windowsill and cleaned its face with its feet.

'Are you all right?' Henry asked. 'You didn't hurt your head, did you?'

'Eh? What? Who said that?' said the Fly, looking round. It gave a scream and fell at once into another panic. 'Oh no, a talking bag!' it yelled, having evidently forgotten everything that had just happened. 'Help! Monsters! Help!' And it flew off – fortunately, this time, in the right direction.

'Well, he was no fun at all,' said Henry, thinking the Fly a very silly sort of creature. Caution was one thing, but constant panic seemed to him a waste of a life. Still, it made a good story to tell the others when he got home.

Just then a breeze came in at the window. 'Hello!' it said. 'What have we here?' And it slipped over Henry and ruffled his edges.

Henry laughed. 'Hey, that feels nice. You can do that again!'

'Oh, you can talk, can you?' the Breeze said, ruffling him again.

'Of course I can talk. There's nothing clever about it,' Henry said. '*You're* talking.'

'Well, if you're going to be rude,' said the Breeze, beginning to withdraw.

'No, wait! Don't go! Stay and talk to me. I've been lying here for ages with nothing to do and I'm bored. I've met a butterfly who was too busy to talk and a fly who was too scared to talk. You're the first sensible thing I've met today.'

'Nice of you to say so,' said the Breeze. It moved about the room, touching things thoughtfully, and then returned to Henry. 'How would you like to come for a ride with me?'

'I'd love it!' said Henry excitedly. 'But I'd better not be too long. The lady I belong to might come back for me any time.'

'Belong to?' said the Breeze in great scorn. '*Belong* to? Whatever can you mean? No one belongs to anyone else. We're all free to do as we like.'

'Are we?' said Henry doubtfully.

'Well, I know *I* am,' said the Breeze. 'You've heard the expression *free as the wind*? That's me. I go where I please.'

'Yes,' said Henry, 'but I've never heard anyone say *free as a paper bag.*'

'I'm not surprised, the way you behave,' said the Breeze. 'You should stand up for yourself. Grasp your freedom. Believe me, it's wonderful! Come on, I'll show you.'

'All right,' said Henry, excited by this talk. 'Let's go!'

The Breeze whirled round, shot inside Henry and lifted him up and out of the window and high into the sky.

Just at first Henry was too thrilled by the rush of movement to think of anything at all, except, *I'm flying!* It was a wonderful sensation. He would really have liked to look around, and especially *down*, to see the world from this new angle. But the Breeze was having a fine time playing with him, spinning him round, turning him upside down and

19

back to front, and Henry could see nothing at all but a blurred rush of shapes and colours.

'I s–say, sl–o–ow d–down!' he cried in a wobbly voice, but the Breeze just chuckled.

'Not scared are you?' he said. 'Hold on, cully! Here we go! Whee–e–ee!' And he hurled Henry higher and faster, round and round, until he looped the loop and almost turned inside out.

Henry began to feel rather sick. 'Put me do–o–own!' he wailed. 'Put me *do–o–own!*'

The Breeze grew huffy. 'Oh well, if you're going to make such a fuss about it!' he said. 'Worse than a fly, you are.' He swooped down sickeningly, dropping Henry on the ground. 'There! And I was trying to be nice, giving you an exciting ride.'

'Thank you,' panted Henry, getting his breath back, 'but that was a bit *too* exciting for me.'

'Suit yourself!' said the Breeze, and started to go away.

'Hey!' said Henry. 'Wait! You have to take me back!'

'*I* don't have to do anything,' the Breeze retorted. 'I'm free as the wind, remember? And, now, so are you.'

'But what shall I do?' Henry cried.

'Anything you want,' said the Breeze, and then he really was gone.

That was all very well, Henry thought, but there wasn't very much he *could* do, being only a paper bag. Here he was, all alone on a grass verge beside a road, and he had no idea where he was or how to get home. Freedom, he thought, was not all that the Breeze had cracked it up to be!

Well, he had to do something, so he started off along the grass verge. But his progress was very slow. After a while a car went by, and the wind of its passage caught Henry and blew him several yards further along. His spirits lifted. That was the way he'd get home! Every car that passed would blow him part of the way, and bit by bit he'd get along. He craned up out of the grass to look for the next car.

But it was a quiet road, and a long time passed before another car came along, and blew him a few yards more. At this rate, he thought, it'd be days before he got home.

And the next car after that was going in the other direction, and it blew him backwards! He'd lost several yards of his precious progress! He felt very frustrated.

Then a terrible thought came to him: he wasn't actually sure which direction home was in. Was it that way or this way? Was it forwards or backwards? Despair settled over him. It was hopeless. He would *never* get home! He was wishing like anything now that he had not listened to the Breeze, that he had stayed safely on the table, where the Mother could find him.

He was sunk in his misery when something else came along, humming to itself in a rather muffled way. It was something large and brownish-red and it had a very strong smell about it, something that Henry had never smelt before. It was a fox, and it was carrying half a chicken carcase in its mouth.

The Fox stopped beside Henry, putting down the chicken beside him, to take a rest. It used its paw to clean its whiskers, licked its lips a couple of times, then sighed and muttered to itself, 'Oh, that thing makes my jaws ache!'

'I should think it would,' said Henry politely. 'It looks rather large for your mouth.'

The Fox was startled. It jumped up and looked around. 'Who said that?' Then it looked at Henry. 'It wasn't you, was it? Paper bags don't talk.'

'How do you know?' said Henry. 'Have you ever met a paper bag before?'

'Not a *live* one,' said the Fox, giving him a sidelong look. Henry shivered. He didn't want to think what *that* meant. The Fox's eyes were dark and bright and his teeth were sharp and white. Just for a moment, Henry's paper, which he had always been so proud of, felt very thin and vulnerable.

'What are you doing here, anyway?' the Fox asked him.

'I'm trying to get home. The Breeze brought me this far, but then it dropped me for no reason and just wandered off.'

'Yes, breezes are like that,' said the Fox. 'So unreliable. Here one minute and gone the next. You know where you are with a good strong wind, but a breeze . . .' He shrugged. 'Where do you live, then?' he asked.

Henry told him. 'It's called Honeysuckle Cottage, and it stands all alone at the top of the heath.'

'Oh, yes, I think I know where you mean,' said the Fox. 'I live on the heath myself, but in the middle. I've got a fine lair in a snug little copse.'

Henry grew excited. 'Oh, then do you think you could take me home?'

'Certainly not,' said the Fox. 'I've got quite enough on my plate, with this chicken to get home to my cubs. You'll have to sort out your own problems. I've problems of my own.'

Henry thought of something. 'Yes, I heard you complaining that your jaws ached,' he said.

'So would yours, trying to get a grip on this carcase,' snapped the Fox.

'But look here, how would it be if we helped each other?' said Henry.

'How can *you* help *me*?' the Fox asked rather rudely.

'I could hold the chicken for you, and you could hold me. That would be much easier on your jaws.'

It took the Fox a moment to understand what Henry meant. But foxes are clever creatures, and he soon saw the benefit of the plan. 'All right,' he said. 'I'll do it – but I'll only carry you as far as my lair. I haven't time to go traipsing off all over the heath, with cubs to feed.'

'But I need to get home!' Henry cried.

'Well, it's half way – that's better than nothing, isn't it?'

'I suppose so,' Henry said. 'But how will I know which way to go afterwards?'

'Oh, I'll point you in the right direction, don't worry. Is it a bargain?'

Henry felt he hadn't much choice, so he said yes. He didn't much like the idea of holding the chicken carcase inside him, but it turned out to be very dried out and not too bad after all. Then he told the Fox to take hold of the top of him. 'But be careful with those teeth,' he shouted at the last minute.

The Fox gripped him hard, which was uncomfortable, but not painful. 'Oh, this is much better,' the Fox said through his teeth. 'I can get along much better now.' Henry was glad to hear it.

The Fox trotted off, with Henry swinging a little from his jaws. He plainly knew his way very well, for he travelled swiftly and surely along the hedgerow, under a gate, across a field, and through a hedge on to the heath. Henry was worried about his looks after a journey like this. It wouldn't do for him to get dirty or dishevelled. *I shall look as if I've been pulled through a hedge backwards*, he thought unhappily. But he was certainly making ground, and going in the right direction at last.

Suddenly the Fox dropped him, and Henry, who had been almost in a dream, looked around. There was a copse of trees off to his left, and open heath ahead.

'My lair is in the copse there,' said the Fox, emptying out the chicken carcase. Henry was not sorry to be rid of it. 'You carry on in this direction and you'll get to the top of the heath where the cottage is.'

'Couldn't you just take me the rest of the way?' Henry said. 'Please?' It was no distance for the Fox, but a terrible journey for him.

The Fox was walking away. 'No I could *not*,' he said over his shoulder. And he muttered to himself as he disappeared into the bushes, 'Honestly, hitch-hikers! Never satisfied. No gratitude at all.'

Henry was left alone on the heath. The afternoon was advancing, and he was afraid it would be getting dark soon. And the clouds in the sky looked different. Were they rain clouds? He had heard about rain, and what it could do to paper. If he got wet, he might grow soggy, and split. He might melt away altogether and be nothing but pulp! He shivered. 'Oh, what am I to do?' he said aloud. 'Whatever am I to do?' And he started to struggle along over the rough heathland.

Just then a slice of stale bread fell out of the sky and nearly landed on him. 'Oy!' Henry shouted. 'Look out!' A bird flew down and dropped beside him. It looked at him with its head on one side. 'Was it you that said that?' it asked.

'Was it you that dropped the bread?' Henry retorted crossly. 'You nearly brained me.'

'Sorry,' said the bird. 'I lost my grip on it. It's a bit big, and I couldn't see round it. Nearly flew into a tree. I say, I've never met a talking bag before.'

Henry was getting a bit tired of this reaction. 'I've never met a talking bird,' he said. The bird looked astonished. 'Are you kidding? I'm a starling. We never *stop* talking. It's what we're famous for.'

'Well, bully for you,' said Henry grumpily.

'What's wrong with you?' asked the Starling. 'Are you in trouble?' It was a kindly bird and didn't like to see a fellow creature miserable.

'I'm trying to get home, but as you see I'm finding it rather difficult,' said Henry

'Where do you live?' asked the Starling.

'Honeysuckle Cottage. It's—'

'Oh, I know it,' the Starling interrupted. 'You live there, do you? It's got a smashing ilex tree in the garden, and a hawthorn hedge behind. Both are stuffed with delicious berries in autumn. My mates and I fed there last year. Yum yum!' It rolled its eyes at the memory of the feast.

Hope revived itself painfully in Henry's heart. 'Do you think you could you take me there?'

'I *could*,' said the Starling doubtfully. 'But I was on my way home. That's in the other direction.'

'It wouldn't take you a minute,' Henry pleaded.

'But what's in it for me?' said the Starling. 'There are no berries there now, I know for a fact.'

Henry remembered how they had met. 'Look here,' he said, 'that bread is too big for you to fly with. You could put it in me and carry me instead. That would be much easier.'

The Starling took a minute to think this out. 'Yes, I see what you mean,' it said. 'But look here, if I fly you home with my bread, *you'll* be home, but *I'll* be even further away, and the bread will still be too big for comfort.'

'What if,' said Henry slowly, thinking it out as he spoke, 'what if I tell you how to get the bread home more easily?'

'How?' the Starling asked.

'I'll tell you that when you've flown me home,' said Henry firmly.

The Starling turned his head the other way, and looked at him out of the other eye, to make sure. 'No tricks, now?'

'Of course not,' Henry said with dignity. 'Paper bag's honour.'

So the Starling put the bread inside Henry, took a firm grip on him with its beak, and flew up into the sky. This was a much nicer trip than he had had with the Breeze. The Starling flew straight and steady, and Henry was able to look around and enjoy the view. He saw the whole of the heath, and the roads and paths that crossed it, and there – oh joy of joys! – there was Honeysuckle Cottage on its high point, with the road running by it. He saw the ilex tree the Starling had mentioned – he must remember to tell the others about that – and the hawthorn hedge that divided the back garden from the fields. And he could even see the Mother's car, looking very small from up here, driving along the road a little way off from the cottage. She hadn't got home yet! But she'd be there soon!

Henry was so excited to see her coming. 'Put me down just by the front door!' he called to the Starling. The bird swooped and dropped and in a moment had landed beside the empty milk bottles. Henry hurried to tip out the bread. 'Go, go quickly,' he said. 'The Mother is coming! I want her to find me, but you won't want to be here.'

'No,' said the Starling with a shudder. 'Humans are good for throwing out bread, but I like to keep a good distance between them and me.'

'Fly away then,' Henry said, because he could hear the car coming now. 'Hurry!'

'But you haven't told me how to get the bread home,' the Starling said. 'I warned you about not tricking me!' It made a threatening movement with its sharp beak.

'Oh, I never meant to trick you,' said Henry. 'I'm very grateful for the lift. To get the bread home more easily, all you have to do is eat half of it. Then it will be smaller and easier to carry.'

'Well, I never!' said the Starling. 'I hadn't thought of that. You *are* a clever fellow.' At that moment the Mother's car came round the corner and pulled up in front of the cottage. 'Oops! Got to go!' said the Starling. 'I'll do the eating somewhere else, where it's safe. So long! See you in the autumn, maybe.'

'Goodbye!' Henry called after the Starling as it flew off, with the bread in its beak like a big white envelope. 'Take care! Good luck with it.'

And then all he had to do was to straighten himself as best he could, and wait. In a moment, the Mother came up to the door, pulling her keys out of her bag.

'Hello, what's this?' she said, stooping to pick up Henry. He was so glad to be in her hand again that he trembled all over with pleasure and relief. 'Good gracious,' she said as she examined him. 'It looks like the same bag. But it can't be . . .' And he could see that she was trying to think it out, knowing that she had last seen him on her friend's table, miles away. Then she shrugged the problem away. 'Oh well,' she said. 'I suppose one bag is much the same as another.'

Very soon after that he was in the house and being put back into the dresser drawer in the familiar warm darkness. The other bags were excited to see him.

'Where have you been?'

'What was it like?'

'Did you have an adventure?'

'Didn't I just!' said Henry, and settled down to tell them, for what was to be only the first time, all that had happened to him. And as he told his story, he thought that for once the Mother was quite wrong. One bag was definitely *not* the same as another!

Henry and the Picnic

One summer day, Henry was taken out of the drawer, and found the kitchen a hive of activity. Food of all sorts was spread across the kitchen table. The little girls, Betty and Polly, were in a state of great excitement, and Henry thought perhaps a party was in preparation. But he listened hard to their chatter, and heard a new word – 'picnic'. He didn't know what it meant, but it seemed to be making them rush round the kitchen and talk at the tops of their voices. They were doing their best to help the Mother prepare for this treat, but they seemed only to be adding to the confusion.

One of the other paper bags, Gordon – a plain brown bag who had first arrived in the house carrying plums from the farmers' market – had also been taken out. He seemed to know a bit more than Henry about the situation, and explained what a 'picnic' was.

'Haven't you ever heard of it before?' he said, rather scornfully. 'It means they get a lot of grub together – sandwiches and suchlike – and take it out in the car with them.'

'And then what?' asked Henry.

'They sit down in a field and eat it, of course,' said Gordon.

'Oh,' said Henry. 'And what else?'

'Well,' said Gordon, thinking hard. He was enjoying the experience of knowing more than a posh bag like Henry, and he racked his brain for more details. 'Well, the kids play games, and muck about. They might go swimming, if they're having the picnic by a river or by the sea. The grown-ups talk a bit and generally fall asleep. And then they pack everything up and come back home.'

'I see,' said Henry, doubtfully. 'What do they do it for?'

'It's the eating, I suppose,' said Gordon. 'Makes a nice change for them, eating out of doors.'

'Oh, yes, I can see that,' said Henry. 'Well, it sounds nice.' And he was glad to have been chosen to go along with the family. He thought there was probably more to it than what Gordon had said – he didn't have a great opinion of Gordon's intelligence. But in any case he loved adventures of any sort, he loved driving in the car, and he looked forward most of all to telling the others about it afterwards when he was back in the drawer.

He hoped Gordon would let him be the one to tell the story, and not hog all the attention to himself. Gordon liked to talk. By now everyone in the drawer knew everything there was to know about farmers' markets – or at least, everything Gordon knew about them, which was probably not the same thing.

While the preparations were going on, some other children arrived, friends of Betty and Polly, who were to go on the picnic with them.

31

The Mother told the little girls to take their friends into the sitting room to play while she finished preparing.

Soon the food was all ready, and the Mother began to wrap it up and pack it into a big wicker basket. It all looked lovely. There were egg-and-cress rolls and beautiful red tomatoes, warm and sweet from the garden. There were cold sausages, with tomato sauce to dip them in. There were sausage rolls and little pork pies. There were home-made pasties with pale golden pastry, the edges crimped together along the top like the frill on a party dress, and filled with savoury meat and potatoes. There were jellies in little clear plastic bowls, looking like jewels as the sun shone through them: ruby red and amethyst purple and emerald green. There were fairy cakes with different coloured icing on them – pale yellow and pale pink and pale green – and each had a little silver ball in the very centre. There were gingerbread men, with their faces piped on in icing, and currants for buttons all down their fronts. There were Victoria plums, purple and pink and yellow, with the bloom still on them. There was lemonade to drink, and the Mother was filling a big Thermos flask with hot tea for herself.

Now, Polly didn't like egg-and-cress rolls. She liked eggs hot at breakfast, but not hard-boiled and cold. So the Mother had made her a cheese sandwich, and Henry was given the job of carrying it. It came in two halves, and the halves were triangular and looked almost identical. But then Henry noticed that one of them had a slightly rounded top edge. It said its name was Verso, while the other, whose edges were all quite straight, said its name was Recto.

When they had been put into Henry and Henry had been packed

into the hamper with the rest of the containers, the hamper was carried out to the car. The children climbed in, chattering and laughing, and the hamper was put into the boot, along with the picnic rug and a large blue-and-red ball and a yellow frisbee. Henry was disappointed when the boot lid was closed, because it became quite dark. He loved to ride in the car, but on this occasion he wouldn't be able to see anything.

They started off. Despite the noise of the engine, Henry could hear the cheese sandwiches talking. Since he had nothing else to do, he began idly to listen to what they said. They were very excited about the picnic, but Henry soon realised that Verso and Recto had no more idea what a picnic was than he himself had had until Gordon had explained it.

'I think it's a kind of game,' said Verso.

'No, I think it's more of a place,' said Recto. 'Something like a shop, maybe. A bakery or a dairy most likely,' he added, since those were the sorts of shops he liked best.

'Well, if it's a place, maybe it's a place where things like games happen. I heard once about something called a circus, which sounded very exciting,' said Verso.

'It's very nice of them to take us along,' said Recto. 'Very thoughtful, I call it. They obviously want us to enjoy ourselves.'

'Of course they do,' said Verso. 'I heard that little girl saying she *loved* cheese sandwiches, and the Mother said that she did too. I expect the whole thing was arranged as a treat for us.'

Now Henry had been listening without much interest at first. But as time went on he began to feel rather uncomfortable. It was his duty to keep the cheese sandwiches safe and clean for the family. The

Mother herself had given them to him, which meant it was his sacred duty to look after them.

But it was plain that Verso and Recto hadn't the faintest idea what was in store for them, and he began to feel that perhaps he ought to warn them. It seemed unkind to let them go to their fate all unknowing. On the other hand, he argued with himself, perhaps it was better for them not to know?

But they were so happy and excited about the whole thing that in the end he felt he had to say something.

By now they had settled down to asking, 'Are we there yet? Are we there yet?'

He interrupted this at last to say, 'Look here, you two, I wouldn't get too worked up about this picnic, you know.'

'Oh,' said Verso, 'do you know what it is, then?'

'Yes,' said Henry, 'I do. It's a sort of human thing where they take lots of food out into the country.'

'Oh yes?' said Recto brightly. 'That sounds nice. I like the country.'

'So do I,' said Verso. 'We're country people really, you know. Cheese comes from milk, which comes from cows, and cows live in the country.'

'And bread comes from wheat,' said Recto, 'and wheat grows in the country.'

'Yes, yes,' said Henry impatiently, 'I dare say it does.'

'So the countryside is very *us*,' said Verso.

'It's nice of the humans to take us along,' said Recto.

'Well, up to a point,' said Henry, feeling very uncomfortable now.

'So what happens when we get there?' asked Verso brightly. 'It's a kind of game, isn't it? I bet it's a kind of game!'

34

'Not exactly,' said Henry. 'They – er – they unpack everything—'

'Yes?' said Verso.

'And spread out a blanket—'

'Yes?' said Recto.

'And lay out all the food—'

'Like us, you mean?'

'Yes,' said Henry. 'Like you.'

'And then what?'

'And – er – and then they – er – they eat it.'

'They eat the blanket?' said Verso.

'No, they eat the food,' said Henry.

There was a long, terrible silence.

'They eat *us*?' said Recto in a horrified voice.

'Um – yes, I'm afraid so,' said Henry.

There was another silence.

'*Why did nobody tell us?*' said Recto wildly.

'Well, I suppose—' Henry began.

'You've got to do something,' Verso interrupted decidedly. 'You've got to save us.'

'But I don't know how.'

'Think of something!' said Recto. 'You can't let us be eaten.'

'Well, I'll do my best,' Henry said, though for the moment he couldn't see what he could do.

'You were chosen to be our guardian,' said Verso. 'We're depending on you. You're so clever, I just know you'll find a way.'

'Right,' said Henry, and sank into thought. They were depending on him, but he hadn't the least idea what he could do about it.

The car stopped and the boot lid was opened, and through the sides of the hamper Henry could see that they were in the open country, with fields and hedges and trees around them. The Mother lifted out the hamper while the children took the blanket and playthings, and soon they were settled in a wide field which sloped downwards from the road at the top to a wood at the bottom. The blanket was spread out, they all sat down, and then the hamper was opened and the Mother began lifting out the bags and containers of food. Henry saw that it was a lovely sunny day, with a fine blue sky above, lightly fretted with clouds. There were lots of wild flowers dotted about, with butterflies flitting among them. The grass where they were sitting was short and full of clover, and there were bumble bees wandering from one tight, honey-packed head to another. But further down the field, towards the wood, the grass was rougher and longer. A light wind was fooling about with it, having fun by making it bend over and then letting it go so that it sprang up straight again.

It was this that gave Henry his idea.

'Listen,' he said to Verso and Recto, 'I'm going to create a diversion. When the moment comes, you must be ready to run. When I say the word, run like mad down the hill towards the trees. You can hide in there. After that, it's up to you.'

Verso and Recto said they'd be ready. Then Henry called to the wind:

'I say, can I have a word with you?'

The Wind drifted over to him. 'Howdy, pardner,' it said – for it was a westerly wind. 'Kin I do sumthin' for ya?'

'Yes,' said Henry, and he explained his plan. 'Will you do it?' he asked.

'Sure, why not?' said the Wind. 'I guess them little critters don't wanna get eaten, no sirree! Let's you an' me have us a piece a fun!'

'Right,' said Henry. 'When I say the word, then.'

He watched carefully for his chance. The Mother had finished getting all the food out of the hamper, and now she reached for Henry, took the cheese sandwiches out of him and laid them on a paper plate. This was his moment.

'Now!' he shouted to the Wind, and opened his mouth as wide as he could. The Wind shot up inside him and snatched him out of the Mother's hand, lifting him up into the air.

'Oh no!' cried the Mother, trying to catch him.

The Wind blew enthusiastically, whirling Henry higher. 'Yippee!' he whooped. 'Ride 'em up!

'Not too high,' Henry said. 'We want her to chase me, not give up.'

'Quick!' the Mother cried to the children. 'Catch the bag! We mustn't let it get away.'

All the children jumped up, thinking it a fine bit of fun. All eyes were on Henry, all hands reached out for him. He shouted down to the cheese sandwiches, 'You two! Run! Quick, quick, run!'

He was glad to see that they acted at once, dashing off the plate and off the rug and across the grass as fast as they could. Meanwhile, the Wind was having a wonderful time playing with Henry, teasing his pursuers, letting them almost catch him, and then snatching him up and away again. He led them a fine old dance, keeping Henry always just out of reach, leading them further and further away from the picnic blanket, until they were all breathless with running and laughing.

From his vantage point, Henry saw that Verso and Recto had reached the edge of the wood at the bottom of the slope, and were disappearing into the trees. 'Good luck,' he murmured, and hoped that fate would be kind to them. Then to the Wind he said, 'It's all right, you can let me down now.'

'Aw, shucks, I was havin' such a good time,' said the Wind, but he slipped out of Henry all the same, and Henry drifted down until he came low enough for the Mother to catch hold of him.

'Thanks a lot,' Henry called to the Wind.

'Any time, li'l pardner,' the Wind replied, and blew away to look for some leaves to rustle. Being a westerly wind, it was keen on rustling.

The Mother and the children went back to their picnic, with an appetite improved by all the running about. 'Always remember, children,' the Mother said, 'that you must never leave any litter behind when you go out in the country. You must make sure to take everything back with you when you go home.'

Henry didn't much like being referred to as 'litter', but he was very glad to hear this rule all the same, and thought it a very sound principle. He was pleased that the sandwiches had got away, but he didn't want to be left out in a field himself. He wanted to go home to his nice cosy drawer.

When everyone was settled down on the rug again, the Mother was mystified to discover that the cheese sandwiches were missing. What could have happened to them?

'Did they blow away?' said Betty, staring around her.

'Of course they didn't,' said the Mother. 'They'd be too heavy to blow away. Besides, the paper plate's still here.'

'Someone must have taken them,' said Polly.

'But there's no one here but us,' said the Mother.

'Maybe a dog came by while we were chasing the bag,' said another little girl.

'Or a fox,' said a boy.

'Or a pixie,' said Betty.

'Don't be daft, there's no such things as pixies,' said the boy.

'I bet there is,' said Polly, 'and I bet they took the sandwiches and ran away.'

In the end, because she could not think of any better explanation, the Mother decided that it must have been a stray dog that had sneaked up out of the hedge, grabbed the sandwiches, and slipped away again.

So everyone settled down to enjoy the rest of the picnic. Polly had an extra sausage roll and an extra pork pie to make up for not having her sandwiches. When they had eaten all they wanted, they played with the ball and the frisbee. The children hoped that if there *was* a stray dog, it would reappear so that they could play with it. They kept a sharp eye out for it. But of course, no dog came.

At last the shadows began to lengthen, and the Mother said it was time to go home. They packed everything up, being very careful to collect up all the paper bags and anything else that might be called litter, and soon they were on their way home in the car. At the picnic place you would never have known they had been there, except that there was one place where the grass was flattened.

Henry dozed a little in the hamper on the way home. In-between dreaming about flying, he thought of the story he would have to tell when he got back to the drawer.

But the best story of all, he thought, would be the adventures that Verso and Recto must be having. He wished he knew what had happened to them! And he wondered all the way home where they were and what they were doing.

Perhaps one day he would find out.

Colin and the Great Green Carrier

Much of a paper bag's life is uneventful, and to pass the time, they love to tell stories. When Henry had been in the dresser drawer for a while, he felt he had heard pretty well all the stories everyone had to tell, both true and made up. Everyone had had an adventure of some kind, and though not every one was equally exciting, a good storyteller could make it sound so.

But there was one paper bag there, a very small paper bag, named Colin, who never seemed to speak at all. And one day, when there was nothing much going on, Henry asked him if he had ever had an adventure.

Before Colin could answer, Gordon, the rough brown bag from the farmers' market, said, 'Oh, he won't have anything worth telling. Look at the size of him! He's too small to be any use to anyone.' He laughed rudely, and several other bags joined in.

Henry thought Colin must be hurt by the mockery, and he was prepared to jump to his defence. But Colin only smiled mysteriously,

41

and said, 'You'd be surprised. Size is not the only thing that matters.'

Henry was impressed by Colin's manner, and intrigued by what he had said. So when things had quietened down, he asked Colin to tell them his story.

'Well, I've never told anyone before,' Colin said doubtfully. But Henry begged him in the nicest way, and finally Colin gave in.

This is the story he told.

Once upon a time, a very small paper bag named Colin lived in the sample room of a paper bag factory. This was the place where people like shopkeepers, who needed paper bags for their business, came to see what sorts of bag there were, and choose the kind that was right for them. So there were bags of all sizes and shapes and colours in the sample room for the people to pick from; but the smallest of them all was Colin. He was really, really tiny.

He was not a happy little bag, because the others all made fun of him. 'What use are you?' they would say. 'You could put all sorts of things in *us*, but *you're* too small to hold *anything*!'

They laughed at him and called him names like Titchy and Midget. They told him again and again that he was useless. The bigger, stronger bags used to bully him, too, shoving him out of the way, knocking him over, sitting on him. He got jostled to the back when a customer came in to look at bags, and sometimes the bullies pushed him right off the shelf so that he fell to the floor and got dusty.

Perhaps because of this, or perhaps because he was so small, no customer had ever chosen Colin as the sample of what they wanted. No one had ever looked at him and said, 'There, that's the one! That's exactly the size and shape I need!' And so Colin came to believe that the bullies were right, and that he really was no use at all.

Things had gone on in this unhappy way for a long time. One day Colin was sitting in a corner feeling miserable when Bertie came up to him. Bertie was the only bag who was nice to Colin. Though he was not very big, Bertie was never bullied like Colin. He was popular with the other bags, who respected him because he was just the right size for a lot of different things, so customers often picked him out.

Bertie felt sorry for Colin; and also, he secretly rather admired him, for Bertie was just plain brown paper, while tiny Colin was white with gold stars.

'What's up, young 'un?' he asked Colin on this particular day.

'Oh – the usual,' said Colin with a sigh.

'The others bullying you?' said Bertie. 'You ought to stand up for yourself more.'

'But how can I?' Colin said. 'Look at me. I'm the smallest bag in the whole place.'

'You're much better-looking than me,' said Bertie.

'But what good is that?' Colin cried. 'I'm too small to be used for anything. You couldn't put books in me, or buns, or bananas. I couldn't hold screws or Sellotape or sultanas. The others call me useless, and they're right: not one customer has ever picked me out. Not one! My whole existence is pointless.' And if paper bags could cry, he would have cried then.

Bertie was upset. Though not one of the very brightest, he was a kindly soul, and he hated to see a fellow bag so miserable. He wanted to comfort little Colin, but he couldn't think how to do it.

He said slowly, 'Well, you know, I reckon everyone's good for something. Bound to be.' He stared at Colin and a flash of genius came to him. 'Look here,' he said, 'they wouldn't have made you so beautiful, with lovely gold stars and all, if you weren't *for* something. All you've got to do is to find out what it is.'

'Thanks, Bertie,' Colin said. 'It's nice of you to say so. But even if I *do* have a use, I don't know how to find out what it is.'

Two flashes of genius in one day were too much to expect of Bertie, who had never even had *one* before. But something magical must have been in the air, for he *did* have another one, right there and then. Out of the blue, he heard himself saying, 'You ought to go and ask the Great Green Carrier.'

Colin stared at him in surprise, but it was nothing to Bertie's astonishment at the cleverness of his own words.

'The Great Green Carrier?' said Colin. 'But surely he doesn't really exist? I thought it was just a myth – a story.'

'Oh no, he exists all right,' said Bertie. 'My cousin's got a friend whose brother knows someone who's actually *met* him.'

Colin could hardly believe it. 'The Great Green Carrier?' he said. 'The Fount of All Wisdom? The Great and Mighty One who knows the Answers to All Questions? He *met* him?'

'That's right,' said Bertie, pleased at the effect he was having. 'This chap – the pal of my cousin's friend's brother – he went on a pilgrimage to the Remote Regions. Saw him face to face. Asked him something or other. Mind you, my cousin's friend says his brother told him this pal was never the same afterwards. Went a bit peculiar. Lost his mind. Well, I suppose seeing the Mighty

One in real life must be a bit of a shaker. Still – it's a thought.'

'It's certainly that,' said Colin. 'Thanks, Bertie.'

Colin did think about it a lot in the next few days. He had always assumed the Great Green Carrier was imaginary, one of those tall stories that were told at night when the lights were out and paper bags got together in the dark and chatted. Paper bags like nothing more than a good story, and if it's good enough, they don't much mind whether it's entirely true or not. The taller the better, as long as it's exciting: that's what a paper bag would say.

The idea that there really *was* a Great Green Carrier, who could Answer All Questions, made Colin think long and hard. If he, Colin, did have a purpose in life, if he had been made for a reason, surely the Great Green Carrier would know what it was.

He began to ask around – very casually, because he did not want to be laughed at. He discovered that some of the paper bags thought the same as he did, that there was no such person as the Great Green Carrier. But most did believe in him, some of them very earnestly indeed.

Little by little Colin gathered snippets of information which he added to his own vague ideas, until he had a pretty good picture in his mind.

The Great Green Carrier, it seemed, lived in the Remote Regions, far away on the Highest Shelf, up by the ceiling. He was guarded by the fabled Gatekeeper, an austere and powerful black bag of grim aspect, who turned all but the most earnest seekers after truth away. But before you even reached the Gatekeeper, you had to pass through the regions guarded by the Brotherhood of the Gift Carriers: mighty bags of sumptuous beauty, who had magical powers. It was their task to decide who might be permitted to climb onwards to the Highest Shelf, and to punish those who wasted their time.

As to the Mighty One himself, Colin gathered that he lived in a cave of Mystical Light, which burned day and night even when all else was dark, and that strange and wonderful music could be heard coming from the cave, music so beautiful it could drive a humble bag out of his senses. Of those who tried to see the Great Green Carrier, many fell by the wayside, and of the few who ever entered the cave and saw him face to face, none returned as they had once been. Many simply disappeared; others were struck dumb or lost their wits. Because of that, it was a desperate venture, not to be undertaken lightly.

As to Bertie's cousin's friend's brother's pal, Colin discovered that he never actually made it past the first of the Brotherhood. He'd been too scared to go on. He had made up a good story afterwards, of course, but that's all it was. Colin never told Bertie, not wanting to upset him.

It was a terrible decision for Colin to take, and for a long time he did not think he had the courage. But when the worst of the bullies discovered he had been asking questions, they teased and taunted him even more, until his life was unbearable. So he resolved at last that he must find out, once and for all, what his life meant. He would find the Great Green Carrier, and ask him – even if he perished in the attempt.

Better to die trying, he thought, than to continue in this miserable way. And so one day, very early in the morning, before anyone was awake, he set off.

It was a hard climb for a tiny bag. First he had to cross the floor from the cabinet where he lived, and climb up the cabinet opposite, trying not to wake anyone as he passed. Then he began to climb the shelves. The Highest Shelf, right up by the ceiling, was so far above him that he could see nothing of it. It made him dizzy just to look up there. He shivered a little to think of these Remote Regions, and what they might be like.

As he climbed higher, he left the cheerfulness of the crowded sample room behind him. There were fewer bags up here, and they were a silent and surly lot, living alone far from civilisation. Many of them seemed in a deep slumber, and he was afraid to wake them as he tiptoed past, for fear of what they might do to him.

Then he came to a completely empty shelf. He had never seen such a thing before, and it was a strange, frightening, barren place. The old, scarred wood was thick with dust, in which he could see strange marks like ancient runes. He wondered if they were messages left by pilgrims who had passed that way before, and if so, what they meant. He felt very alone, and wondered if he had the courage to go on. He wanted to hurry back down to his own cabinet and the other bags. Even if they weren't his friends, at least they were familiar, and their presence was comforting.

While he was dithering, he heard a tiny, secretive sound behind him. He whirled round and almost jumped out of his skin. There behind him was a little creature covered in grey plush, with round beady eyes, large pink ears and a long pink tail. It stopped when he turned, and sat up on its hind legs to look at him.

'Hello–ello–ello,' said the Mouse – for that's what it was. 'What are you doing here? I haven't seen anyone on this shelf for a long time.'

'I'm – I'm on a pilgrimage to the Remote Regions,' Colin stammered, for he wasn't sure if the Mouse was dangerous or not. He had heard stories of mice chewing up paper bags to line their nests.

But this Mouse only looked at him with interest. 'Are you, then?' he said. 'But you're a small one. I don't think I've ever seen a bag as small as you.'

'That's why I'm going,' said Colin with some bitterness. 'Everyone says I'm useless. I thought that if anyone could tell me if there's a reason for my existence, it would be the Great Green Carrier. If he exists.'

The Mouse began to chuckle. 'Oh, he exists all right!' he said.

'Are you sure?' asked Colin.

The Mouse grinned, and ran his paws quickly over his whiskers as if to hide his smirk. 'Oh yes. He lives at the furthest end of the Highest Shelf. He's the Fount of All Wisdom, he is!'

'You're making fun of me,' Colin said.

'No, no,' the Mouse grinned, his shoulders shaking with giggles. 'I'm not laughing at you, lad. It's just – s–something I thought of.'

'Well, you won't put me off,' Colin said stoutly. 'I'm going to find him, whatever anyone says.'

The Mouse pulled himself together. 'That's the spirit,' he said. 'It's a long journey for a little 'un like you, though. I hope you make it all right. Keep straight on up, and don't stop for anyone, that's my advice.'

And with a nod and a bright, laughing look, the Mouse went on his way, pattering quickly, keeping close to the wall. Colin noticed that his little naked feet, and his long naked tail, made tiny marks and squiggles in the dust. So they were not ancient runes after all, he thought, just the Mouse's footprints. Or – *were they*? Who knew what anything might mean or not mean in this strange place, so far from home?

He climbed on, past more empty shelves, whose far ends were shrouded in shadow, so that there was no knowing what might be lurking there. He passed great cobwebs, festooned like curtains. He saw dust bunnies as big as himself. He saw more mouse tracks, and the track of something a lot bigger that he did not even want to think about. He became very weary and more and more lonely and frightened. But he was determined to go on, and the further he went, the less he felt he could turn back.

So at last he came up on to a shelf that was not empty. He stopped, not only to catch his breath, but to stare in amazement at what was before him. All along the shelf there were paper bags, but bags of such magnificence as he had never seen before, or dreamed could exist. They were all shapes and sizes – though even the smallest was six times the size of him – and they were all made of some gloriously shiny paper that reflected the dim light like polished metal. The colours were sumptuous – scarlet, purple, gold, silver, deep green, cerulean, puce – and they were decorated with stars and moons, stripes and zigzags, leaves and berries and flowers. They must be, he decided, the most beautiful bags in the whole world. No wonder they had a shelf all to themselves, so far from the floor!

Each of them had beautiful neat handles made of soft matching woven cord, which marked them out as Carriers, the elite of the paper bag world. He guessed that he had reached the Region of the Brotherhood of the Gift Carriers.

What did strike him as slightly odd was that they were all fast asleep, sprawled out in positions of deep relaxation, and several of them were snoring in a very unglamorous way.

He didn't quite know what to do. He couldn't get past them, since they were blocking the whole shelf; and in any case, he didn't feel he ought to try, if they were here to guard the way. On the other hand, he was afraid to wake them. Might they not be very angry, and smite him down with their magic powers? He stood, trembling, wondering what to do, until some dust, disturbed by a particularly fruity snore from a shining purple Carrier, unfortunately tickled Colin and made him sneeze.

It was a huge and explosive sneeze, and at once the Carrier nearest him – a silver one – began to stir.

'Eh? What? Wazzat?' he mumbled. He sat up slowly, still fuddled with sleep. 'What? Did you say something? I was asleep. Who are you?'

'I'm sorry,' Colin said.

'Sorry?' said the Carrier. 'That's a queer sort of name, even for a little bag like you.'

'Oh – no, I'm sorry I woke you. My name's Colin. I've come from the cabinets below, on a pilgrimage to see the Great Green Carrier.'

'The what? The who?' The Silver Carrier seemed much astonished. He woke up fully and examined Colin very carefully and solemnly. 'Now look here, sonny, you can't be serious.'

'But I am,' said Colin. 'I really must see him. It's important.'

'Well, I don't know about that,' said the Silver Carrier in great perplexity.

But now the next Carrier along was stirring. 'What's all the racket about?' he mumbled. 'Vivian, is that you? Talking in your sleep again?'

'No, Sebastian,' said Vivian. 'I'm wide awake. There's someone here wants to see the Mighty One.'

Sebastian sat up and stared at Colin. 'What, *him*?' he said – rather rudely, Colin thought. He nudged the next Carrier in turn – the purple one with the huge snore. 'Here, Marmaduke, wake up. We've got a pilgrim – or so Vivian says. You've got to have a look at this.'

Marmaduke woke Lancelot, and Lancelot woke Peregrin, and so on until all the Brethren were awake. They all stared at Colin and discussed him with great astonishment and without even bothering to lower their voices. Colin began to feel rather annoyed. The Brotherhood might be gorgeous to look at, and have posh names and speak with posh voices, but he thought they were very rude and rather stupid, and he wondered whether they could really have magical powers as he'd been told they had.

51

'Look here,' he said at last, in a loud voice to catch their attention, 'will you let me by or won't you? I've been told you are the first guardians, and I have to pass you in order to get to the Gatekeeper.'

All the twittering conversation stopped as though cut off with a knife. They looked at him nervously.

'I say, you know,' said Sebastian, 'you oughtn't just to say his name like that. He's a Black Bag of a very high order. It takes years of dedicated study and self-sacrifice even to reach the First Level, and he's already at the Ninth. We – er – we actually never say his name out loud at all. We just call him – well – *him*.'

'All right, whatever you say,' said Colin. 'But can I see him?'

'Look here, old chap,' said Marmaduke kindly, 'you don't really want to do that. A little fellow like yourself? One sight of *him* would probably strike you rigid with fear, and if he spoke to you – well, you'd go gibbering mad. Much better go on home, back where you belong.'

'But I can't,' said Colin. 'I *have* to go on. I *have* to see the Great Green Carrier – though I don't suppose it will be any good,' he added sadly. 'How could I bear the sight of the Mighty One, if even the Gatekeeper is so terrifying?'

They all winced in unison as Colin said the name again.

Peregrine turned to Lancelot and lowered his voice – though not enough, for Colin could still hear. He said, 'Can't we get rid of this chap and get back to sleep? I was having a smashing dream.'

'That's all very well,' said Lancelot, 'but you know if we pass anyone who shouldn't be passed, *he'll* be down on us like a ton of bricks.'

This thought impressed the other Carriers. They all began to murmur.

'You're right,' said Everard with a shudder. 'I can do without having to see *him* in a temper.'

'On the other hand, if this chap's really determined . . .' said Roderick.

'Yes – and we stop him . . .' said Julian thoughtfully.

'There'd be even more trouble,' said Tristram.

'We'd better find out,' Sebastian concluded. He cleared his throat, turned to Colin, and said firmly, 'Anyone who wants to pass this place on the way to the Remote Regions has to take a test. We can't let just anyone through, you know.'

'Very well, what is the test?' asked Colin.

They all looked at each other nervously. 'Er – well – er it's more a question, really,' said Sebastian.

'What is it, then?' Colin asked.

More nervous looks, and then they all got together in a huddle, and there was a buzz of inaudible but very puzzled conversation. It was plain none of them knew what the question was. Colin began to feel these were very stupid Brethren indeed.

At last the buzzing stopped, and they shoved Peregrine forward. 'He's going to ask you the Question,' they said.

Peregrine looked very awkward and foolish. 'Er – um – well, the Question, the one all pilgrims have to answer—'

'Yes?' said Colin.

Peregrine pulled himself together and became stern. 'You understand that you have to satisfy us that you are really sincere in your wish to see the Mighty One?'

'Yes, I understand,' said Colin.

'So the Question you must answer is—'

'Yes?'

'Is—'

'Yes?'

'The Question is – do you really, *really* want to see him?'

'Yes, I do,' said Colin solemnly.

'*Honestly?*'

'Honestly,' said Colin.

'All right then,' said Peregrine, looking relieved that it was all over.

Colin stared. 'That was the question, was it?'

'Er – yes. That was it. And you came through with – er – flying colours.'

'Yes, jolly good,' said Sebastian. 'You can be on your way now.'

'Off you go,' said Vivian. 'Good luck.'

'Give our respects to *him*,' said Marmaduke.

'And you might say,' Everard added, 'that you thought we did our part of it really well. If you don't mind. If it comes up in conversation. Just so he knows.'

'Yes, so that he knows he needn't worry,' said Sebastian.

'Or come down here,' said Everard with a significant look.

'I'll tell him,' Colin promised solemnly. They stepped back and made room for him to pass, and patted him on the back as he went, wishing him well.

And so he climbed on to the Highest Shelf.

When he reached it, he knew he had come to the ends of the earth, for there was nothing above him now but the Ceiling itself. The Highest

Shelf was in shadow, and seemed quite empty, except for a strange, dim red glow far, far away at the further end. Colin took a quick peek over the side of the shelf, and the world he knew, the regions of the cabinets and the floor, were so far below him he could barely make them out. He could not see the other paper bags, nor hear the friendly sound of their conversation. Up here in the Remote Regions all was unnaturally silent.

But he had come too far to turn back now. He summoned up his courage and started forward. The dust here was thick and undisturbed, without even so much as a mouse track in it. Well, what mouse would dare to tread this hallowed shelf? As he went forward, Colin made his own tiny prints, and it made him realise how long it must have been since the last time a living bag had stepped this way.

Then suddenly, without warning, without his having seen any movement, the Gatekeeper was before him, blocking his path. He knew it was the Gatekeeper because he was huge and black. Colin trembled before him. He was so black that the shadows had hidden him. His paper was strangely matt, so that the light did not seem to want to pick him out at all, but slid off him and fell away defeated. It was hard to look at him, hard to understand what he might be, this being who lived in this strange, remote place, guarding one who was even mightier than himself.

After what seemed like hours of silence, the Gatekeeper spoke in a faint, whispery voice like the sound of the wind blowing dead leaves across the floor of a ruined church.

'Who are you?'

'I'm Colin,' said the little bag in a shaky voice, and then added, to be on the safe side, 'if you please, sir.'

'Why have you come to the Remote Regions? Don't you know no bag can live here? It is too cold and empty, too dark. The air is too thin, and the fall –' his voice became a downward sigh – 'the fall is certain death.'

'I wasn't meaning to live here, sir,' said Colin, though his knees were knocking. If no bag could live here, then *what was the Gatekeeper*? 'I want to see the Great Green Carrier, to ask him a question.'

The Gatekeeper said nothing.

Colin waited until he felt as if the dust were settling on him, and then said, timidly, 'So, please, may I go and see him?'

'*No*,' came the answer in a ghostly sigh. The Gatekeeper seemed to be fading before Colin's eyes, though as it was so difficult to see him at all, it was hard to tell. '*Go home, little bag, before it's too late.*'

Colin thought of the terrible journey he had undergone, and how far it was to go back. He thought of his life down below, the loneliness and despair, and the unkindness of the bullies. He plucked up all his courage and said, 'Not without seeing the Mighty One. I must ask him if there is a meaning to my life. If I go back without an answer, I shall know that there is no meaning – and then I might as well be dead.'

There was another long silence, and then a sigh deeper and heavier and – it seemed – sadder than any he had ever heard. And then the Gatekeeper whispered, '*You have much courage for so small a bag. You may pass – but at your own risk. What happens to you beyond here is out of my control. Be very sure it is what you want before you proceed.*'

'I'm sure,' said Colin, though all this talk was giving him the heebie-jeebies, and he'd never felt less sure of anything in his life.

The Gatekeeper seemed to melt into the shadows, and Colin walked past. At least, he assumed he walked past. There was nothing to see, and nothing to hear, only a space that seemed a little colder and stiller than the surrounding air.

He walked towards the dim, red glow at the far end of the Shelf; and as he grew closer, he began to hear a faint humming sound. So that much of the legend was true: the Mystical Light and the strange and wonderful music. Well, he had come this far. If they drove him out of his senses, so be it. At least he would have seen the Great Green Carrier with his own eyes before he perished.

And after a longer walk than he could have imagined, he was finally there. The red glow, he discovered, was caused by a piece of red cloth pinned up like a curtain over the end of the shelf, behind which there was a source of light, and the humming sound, quite loud now. *When I pass that curtain*, Colin thought, *my life will change for ever*. Trembling, he reached out and pulled it aside.

The humming sound stopped, and a voice said, 'Oh, hiya!'

Colin was so dazzled that at first he had difficulty seeing. And when he was able to see, he was so frightened he had difficulty in taking it in. But when he had taken a few deep breaths, he realised that he had not been struck dead or mad. He saw that the Great Green Carrier was indeed great, in the sense of very large. He took up all the space at the end of the shelf. And he was very green indeed, made of some shiny paper in a brilliant shade of lime green. The light did not come from his body, but from a light bulb that was screwed into the ceiling above him at the very end of the shelf.

'Hey, kid,' said the Great Green Carrier, 'have you got a name?'

'I'm Colin, oh Mighty One,' whispered the little bag.

'Whatcher, Colin. How's it going?'

A terrible doubt overcame the little bag. 'Are you really the Great Green Carrier? The Mighty One? The Fount of All Wisdom?'

The GGC gave a modest laugh and waved a hand. 'You don't want to take that stuff too seriously, you know.'

Disappointment clamped like an iron hand over Colin's heart. 'But – but—' he stammered.

'All that "mighty one" malarkey – that was Vernon's idea.'

'Vernon?'

'Didn't you meet Vernon? Big, black bag? Lives back there? Not much to say for himself? Oh – he likes to be called the Gatekeeper, so if you see him again, don't tell him I told you his name was Vernon. But he and I go way back.'

'W–way back?' Colin felt too stunned to understand anything.

'We were about the first bags here, and we decided right away we fancied a quiet life. So we bagsied the top shelf for ourselves. It was Vernon's idea to start up all the Great Green Doodah malarkey, as a way of keeping the small fry away – I mean, no offence, Colin, mate, but we didn't want to share the place with a lot of chattering dimwits. You know how it is.'

'I certainly do,' Colin said quietly, thinking of the Cabinet.

'Of course you do. Of course you do. If you've got this far, you must be an OK guy. Anyway, I think poor old Vern's been up here too long, because he's gone a bit peculiar. I reckon he's started to believe his own fairy tales. And it has to be said – *has* to be said – that he's not great company. He never was talkative, and now he hardly says a word from one month to the next. Gets a bit tedious up here, you know, Colin, sport. That's why I've taken up music, to pass the time.'

'Music? Oh, that was you humming, was it?' said Colin.

'Yeah, I'm working my way through the great musicals. Would you like to hear my rendition of *How Do You Solve A Problem Like Maria*?'

'Not really,' said Colin. 'So – look – all the stories about you, they were just stories, then? You aren't the Fount of All Wisdom?'

'Well, I wouldn't like to claim that, no,' said the GGC with a light laugh.

'And you don't know the Answer to All Questions?'

'Dunno. Depends what the question is. But I'll give it a go. Let's hear it.'

'What's the point?' Colin said bitterly. Now he understood why the Mouse had laughed.

'Here, here, come on. There's no need to be like that. I've been in this sample room a long time, you know, and before that I was in the factory manager's office, on the table behind his desk. That's where I learned the music, from his sound system. Nuts about musicals, he was. So I do know a thing or two. I certainly know a heap more than that lot down there,' he added. 'So what's your question, Colin, old mate?'

Colin shook his head sadly. 'I came here to ask you about the meaning of life,' he said.

'Oh!' said the GGC, looking alarmed. 'Um, could you be a bit more specific?'

'All my life,' said Colin, 'the other bags have laughed at me for my size, and told me I'm useless, too small to put anything in. If they're right, then my whole existence is pointless. But part of me went on believing that I *couldn't* have been made for no purpose, and I hoped that the Fount of All Wisdom might be able to tell me what I was for. Only there isn't a Fount of All Wisdom, only you.'

The GGC looked down at Colin with a kindly smile, hating to see a fellow bag brought so low. 'Size isn't everything,' he said quietly. 'You're a jeweller's bag.'

'A what?' Colin looked up in surprise.

'You were made for the jeweller's trade. For small, very valuable items. The most valuable items in the world, like gold, diamonds and so on, are often small, you know, and they go in small bags. If you'd want me to take a guess, I'd say you were meant for holding a ring box. You can't get much more valuable than that.'

Colin looked up at him, and the sensation of hope rising in his heart was almost unbearable. 'Are you serious? You're not just saying that?'

'Would I kid you? Look at you – smart white bag, thick shiny paper, lovely gold stars all over you. Did it never occur to you they wouldn't have made you so posh-looking if you weren't meant for the luxury trade?'

'The luxury trade?'

'That's you, mate. Posh as they come.'

'But – but why has no one ever chosen me?' Colin asked. 'All those humans who come in for bags – they never pick me out.'

'Oh, your time will come. They don't get through so many of your sort as they do the common old bags. You're high-end. The best. Posher even than the Gift Carriers.'

Colin shook his head in amazement. 'I can't believe it. And yet –

I *knew*, deep down, that I couldn't be quite useless. I knew they must have made me for a reason. Oh, thank you, Great Green Carrier!'

'Chris. The name's Chris.' The GGC yawned hugely. 'And now, if you don't mind, mate, I was about have a nap when you burst in. Not that I haven't enjoyed your company . . . Oh, *now* what's up?'

Colin's face had fallen as he thought of the long journey back. And of the mockers and bullies down below. Would they believe him when he told them? Somehow, he doubted it. He had gained the knowledge of the Meaning of Life, but how would it help him when he got back home?

The GGC got it out of him, and laughed. 'Don't you worry. I'll send you back the quick way. And when they see you coming, they'll know you're something special. You're a smart boy – you'll know how to make use of it. Stand just there – like that.' He positioned Colin on the edge of the shelf. 'That's right. Now then—'

He blew. The powerful wind of his breath sent Colin shooting off into space, and he screamed, seeing the terrible distance below him to the floor. For an instant he thought it was treachery. He would plummet to his death! The Great Green Carrier had betrayed him!

But he had forgotten that he was a paper bag, and paper bags don't plummet. The air resistance caught him, and he wafted gently back and forth, gradually sinking lower. After the first shocking moment, he found he was enjoying it. He could even control the direction he moved. Gradually he drifted down, closer to the Cabinet, where the bags were all sitting about and chatting. He was just about to shout to attract their attention, when one of the bags looked up and saw him.

'Hey! It's Colin. He's come back!'

'Look, he's flying!'

The other bags looked up, and the sight of Colin flying down towards them struck them all of a heap. They clamoured, and waved, and shouted to each other in awe and amazement.

'It was true then! He did go and see the Great Green Carrier!'

'It didn't kill him!'

'He's gained magic powers!'

'I wish we'd been nicer to him!'

And the bags who'd been nastiest, the bullies and mockers, held their hands out to him and wailed, 'Oh Colin, forgive us! Oh Mighty Colin, don't be angry with us!'

'Spare us!'

'Do not smite us with your magic powers!'

'We'll do anything!'

'We'll give you the best place in the Cabinet!'

As Colin landed daintily in front of them, they fell to their knees and grovelled to him, and he let them, just for a bit, because it felt so nice after the jeering. Then he said, 'It's all right, everyone. You don't need to kneel. And I won't be smiting anyone – at least,' he added, remembering the GGC's words about knowing how to make use of it, 'not *yet*.'

The bags who hadn't been quite so mean to him gathered round and asked if he had really seen the Great Green Carrier, and what the Remote Regions were like, and a host of other questions – so many of them that it wasn't possible for him to answer any of them; until, in a brief pause, someone called out, 'Did you get your answer, Colin?'

'Yes,' he said, and silence fell. 'I found out the meaning of my life.'

The silence got even deeper. Quietly, and with superb dignity, he said, 'I am a jeweller's bag.'

The whole crowd, with one voice, gave a great sigh of satisfaction.

After that, Colin said, his life was very happy. No one laughed at him or was mean to him; no one bullied him or pushed him off the shelf. Everyone wanted to talk to him. In fact he gained such a reputation for wisdom that the other bags would come and ask him all sorts of questions, and beg him to give judgement in their disputes, and mediate in their quarrels.

And not long after his adventure, a customer came in, and pointed at him and said, 'There, that one. That's exactly what I want.' It was the best day of Colin's life.

That was the story that Colin told the others in the dresser drawer, and it was such a good story that no one much wondered whether it had all happened *exactly* as he told it, or whether perhaps he had embroidered it a little bit. Not that they minded either way – though Henry would have liked to know if *any* of it was true.

When he had finished, Henry said, 'But, Colin, if you were a sample bag in a sample room, how did you get here?'

'Ah,' said Colin, with a mysterious smile, 'that's another story.'

Henry and the Triple Rescue

Henry had come back from a trip with the Mother and was looking forward to getting back in the drawer and telling the others about it. Not that he had done anything very exciting, but things had been quiet lately. There hadn't been any new stories for ages, so everyone would be interested just to hear where he had been.

But as the Mother approached the dresser with Henry in her hand, the telephone rang. The telephone was in another part of the kitchen, and she put Henry down on the top of the dresser while she went to answer it. It was a long call, and she was chatting for ages, but Henry waited patiently, sure she would come back for him when she had finished. But when she put the receiver back, she went straight out of the kitchen, going right past Henry without looking at him. She had plainly forgotten all about him. He called out to her, but she didn't hear him. Human ears aren't attuned to paper bag voices. If they hear them at all, they just think they are rustling.

Oh dear, oh dear, thought Henry. *Now I'm stuck here on top of the dresser*

64

instead of safe in my cosy drawer – and who knows what will happen next?

He began to imagine all the terrible things that might happen to him. He might get knocked on the floor and trodden on, and get horrible dirty footmarks on himself. He might have something spilled on him, which would be even worse. People were always going past the dresser with cups and glasses of things. One of the children might take him and draw on him, or cut him up to make patterns, the way he had seen them do with coloured paper. Only the other day they had cut up a birthday card and stuck the pieces on to a sheet of paper to make a picture. Suppose they wanted stripes for something? His smart blue and white stripes that he was so proud of?

Even if none of those things happened, something might be put on top of him, hiding him from sight so that he was forgotten for ever. And then someone else, who didn't know how much the Mother admired him, might clear him away. *He might even get thrown in the dustbin!*

He was getting himself into such a terrible fret that he didn't notice a bee come flying in at the kitchen window from the garden. He didn't notice it until it landed right on him. Then he jumped and shouted, 'Oh!'

'What's the matter with you?' the Bee asked. 'I didn't hurt you.'

'You startled me,' said Henry. 'I didn't see you coming. Anyway,' he said grumpily, 'there are plenty of other places to sit – why do you have to pick on me?'

'Ooh, we are touchy!' said the Bee. 'It just happens that the sunshine's been falling on you and you're nice and warm. I've been working really hard all morning, and I wanted to rest my wings for a few minutes and wash my face. I thought you looked nice for a sit down. But if you're so particular a person can't even *touch* you . . .' And he made huffy, going-away movements with his wings.

'Oh, no, it's all right,' Henry said, feeling a bit ashamed of his ill humour. 'I don't mind, really. You sit there, and make yourself comfortable. Sorry if I sounded snappy. I'm a bit worried, that's all.'

'Oh yes? Why's that, then?' said the Bee, beginning to clean the golden pollen off its face with its front legs. The fur on its back was thick with it too – it looked like being a long job.

Henry told him about not being put back in his drawer. The Bee didn't seem to think that was much of a problem, until Henry recounted some of the things he had thought of that might happen to him. 'I see what you mean,' said the Bee. 'Especially that bit about the children.' It shuddered. 'I don't like children. Too unpredictable. You never know what they'll get up to next. Actually, I don't much like humans at all, really.'

'Oh, but *my* human is nice,' Henry said, thinking of the Mother. 'She looks after me beautifully.'

'Huh!' said the Bee. 'You think you've got it trained, but you can't rely on it. I've seen it before. They wait until you're off your guard, and then they turn savage.'

'Turn savage?' Henry was taken aback. 'Have you had trouble with humans, then?'

'*Trouble!*' the Bee said, pausing to stare at Henry. 'I should just about think I have!' It went back to its grooming. 'I keep clear of them as much as possible,' it went on, combing its back with a hind leg, 'but sometimes they creep up on you, or you don't realise they're there.

And as soon as they see you, they start screaming. Then it's flap, flap, flap with their arms, or they try to hit you with a newspaper or something and kill you.'

'How dreadful! But why would they want to kill you?'

The Bee looked exasperated. 'Because they can't tell the difference between a bee and a wasp! Or can't be bothered to learn, more like.'

'Oh,' said Henry. 'I see.' Although he didn't, really. 'What *is* the difference between a bee and a wasp?' he asked, and as the Bee buzzed irritably, he said, 'from a human's point of view, I mean. Obviously *I* know you're different.'

The Bee looked at him suspiciously. '*Do* you?'

'Er – well – no, not really,' Henry admitted.

The Bee sighed. 'Another ignoramus! Look, we're entirely different. Your bee is a hard-working, peaceable fellow. We go about our business not bothering anyone, and all we want is to be left alone. But your wasp, now, he's different. He works hard, I don't say he doesn't, but he's a busybodying, interfering sort of chap, always sticking his nose into everyone's business. And then, if you object, he'll sting you.'

'Don't bees sting?'

'Of *course* not,' said the Bee scornfully. 'Don't you know *anything*? If we sting anyone, we die. Can't pull the sting out again, you see. So we make jolly sure *not* to sting, except as a very last resort, defending the hive or something like that. But your wasp, he can sting as often as he likes and no harm to him, so he's not careful about it like us. Sting you as soon as look at you, some of 'em.' It sniffed, and added, 'I've known wasps that actually *enjoy* it. Fly off sniggering, they do. Vulgarians!'

'So the humans think you're a wasp and will sting them?' Henry said. 'I suppose you can't blame them, though.'

'Of *course* I blame them! They could take the trouble to find out what they're dealing with. We don't look anything alike. Besides, they wouldn't have any trouble from wasps, either, if it weren't for their silly habit of eating out of doors.'

'But don't you eat out of doors?' asked Henry.

'Certainly not,' said the Bee with dignity. 'I *collect* my food out of doors, but then I take it home and eat indoors, like a civilised person. All this eating in gardens, and sitting about on blankets in fields, that humans do! Picnics! Huh! No wonder the ants and the wasps come flocking. No one's going to turn down a free meal, are they? And then the humans go mad and start trying to kill everyone.'

'I suppose you're right,' said Henry. 'I hadn't thought about it before. So these wasps are worthless fellows, then? I mean, I know bees make honey, but wasps don't make anything, do they? They're useless.'

'No, that's not true,' said the Bee. 'I don't think any creature is completely useless. I mean, it wouldn't make sense to create something without a purpose, would it? Except,' it added doubtfully, 'the mosquito. I've never found out what *they're* for, except spreading disease. But then, I suppose if you were a disease, you'd *want* to be spread. Maybe diseases think they're wonderful chaps.'

That was getting a bit deep for Henry. He asked, 'So what do wasps do, then?'

'They eat dead wood,' said the Bee. 'And it has to be said they work really hard at it. If it weren't for them, you know, we'd all be chin deep in dead trees.'

'Oh. Well, that's useful, I suppose. What do they do it for?'

'They chew up the wood and mix it with saliva to make paper,' said the Bee. 'Sooner them than me.'

'Paper?' said Henry, with interest. 'Like me – like my sort of paper?'

'Same thing, I suppose, in principle. They make their nests out of it – very artistic, too. Like honeycombs, they are, only shaped in a ball. Ever so pretty. You'd never think, considering what rough, vulgar blokes they are, that they could make anything so dainty. I've seen—'

Just at that moment something heavy came flying down through the air and landed with a thud on Henry. It was an empty glass jam jar, mouth downwards. One of the children had crept up and slammed it down, trapping the Bee inside.

The Bee was furious. It flew up in a rage and yelled, 'Now look what you've done! Kept me talking so I didn't notice 'em coming! You idiot! Now I'm trapped, and it's all your fault!'

'I'm sorry,' Henry said. 'I didn't hear them either.'

They were both there, Betty and Polly, and he saw their faces grow huge as they bent down to stare at the Bee, their noses almost touching the glass. The Bee flung itself at them in fury, buzzing madly and banging its head against the glass, and the children squeaked and jumped back.

'Idiotic, stupid, clot-headed paper bag!' the Bee raged, banging the glass again and again. 'Got me trapped – me! I've kept away from humans all this year and now look! It'll be the rolled-up newspaper next, you'll see. Lemme out! LEMME OUT!'

'I'm sorry, I'm sorry,' Henry said, 'but do shush a minute. I can't hear what they're saying. We need to know what they're going to do next.'

The Bee saw the point of that and landed again on Henry. It sat still and quiet, listening. Henry strained to hear the girls.

'What'll we do now?' Polly was saying.

'We ought to kill it, nasty old wasp,' said Betty.

'I know, but if we lift up the jar it'll get out and bite us,' said Polly.

'Sting us,' Betty corrected.

'Well, it'll hurt, anyway. I don't want to touch it.'

'I know, let's go and get Mummy. She'll know how to kill it,' said Betty, and the two of them went out of the kitchen.

'There you are, you see,' said the Bee furiously. 'They'll bring in this Mummy of theirs and that'll be the end of me!'

'But the "Mummy" they were talking about is my human, and she's nice. I'm sure she wouldn't hurt you,' said Henry.

'Huh! Tell that to my cousin Wilbur. He got squashed last week. I've got to get out of here! You got me into this, *you* think of something.'

'All right, all right, wait a minute,' said Henry.

'I haven't got a minute,' said the Bee. '*Do* something!'

The Bee was walking round and round in circles muttering to itself while Henry racked his brains for an idea. Then he noticed that the Bee's tiny weight was shaking him. It surprised him and he wondered why, and looked more closely at the situation. He saw that when the Mother had put him down on the dresser, part of him had been left sticking out over the edge. If they could only move the jam jar a little closer to the edge, that piece of him would bend downwards when the Bee stood on it, and it would be able to get out under the jam jar's rim.

He explained it all to the angry Bee, who calmed down at the thought that escape might be possible. It walked over to that side of the jar, and the piece of Henry under its feet did bend downwards a little, but not enough to get out.

But Henry had felt the jar tremble.

'That's it!' he said. 'Jump up and down as hard as you can just there, and I'll try and help. It won't take much to overbalance the jar. But be ready to dodge it when it goes, and don't get caught as it falls.'

The Bee did as Henry said, while Henry concentrated on making that loose bit of him that was hanging over the edge vibrate as much as possible. The jam jar was too heavy for him simply to move it, but between them they managed to make it rock a little, and bit by bit it was being jiggled towards the edge of the dresser. Then quite suddenly its mouth passed beyond the edge, it overbalanced and went flying down to crash below on the hard tiles of the kitchen floor.

The Bee had moved smartly, and flown safely out of the way. Now it came back to land on Henry again, looking hugely relieved.

'Thanks,' it said. 'That was a close shave. You're a smart fellow to think of that. I'll try and remember it, if ever I'm caught that way again.'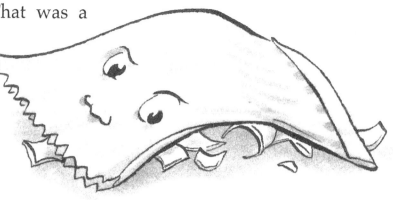

'I hope you won't be,' said Henry. 'But don't hang around here – they'll have heard the crash, and they'll be coming back any moment.'

'You're right. I'd better buzz off,' said the Bee. 'Thanks again – and good luck with getting back into your drawer!' And it flew away and out of the window into the garden.

It was only just in time, for Henry could hear the voices of the little girls approaching, and the next moment the kitchen door was swung open and they came in, exclaiming about the noise.

Now Henry saw a terrible thing. There was broken glass down there on the floor, and the girls had bare feet. But neither of them had noticed the glass. They were too busy looking nervously around for the Bee, wondering whether it was still in the kitchen, and whether it might suddenly attack them. The one place they were not looking at was at the floor, but they were coming closer, and at any moment now one of them might step on the broken glass with her bare foot and cut herself.

There was no time to waste. The draught caused by opening the kitchen door had ruffled Henry, and made him realise what he must do. With an effort born of desperation he propelled himself over the edge of the dresser and planed down towards the floor, using the air movement to guide himself towards the glass. His downward movement seemed agonisingly slow to him, and his fear was that they would reach the glass before he did. But they were too busy looking round for the Bee to hurry, and he managed to get down to the floor and spread himself on top of the glass just in time. Polly's foot had just been hovering over the danger spot, but as she saw Henry there she drew her foot back to safety.

What a save! Henry thought. Now even if they trod on him, he thought his paper would be thick enough to protect them from being cut.

The Mother was coming into the kitchen, too, alerted by the noise of breaking glass. 'What's happening? What are you girls doing?' she asked crossly. 'And what's that bag doing on the floor?'

Before the girls could say anything, she reached down and picked up Henry, and at once saw the broken glass.

'We didn't do it, Mummy,' said Betty.

'It must have just fallen on its own,' said Polly.

'We'd only used it to catch a wasp, but we didn't drop it, honestly.'

Speaking both at once they explained what they had done, and how they had been out of the room when they heard the glass breaking.

'Oh well, I suppose it was an accident,' said the Mother. 'And it was sensible of you to cover the glass up like that. But let's get it cleared up properly now.'

She put Henry back on the dresser and fetched the dustpan and brush, and with the girls' help the glass was all cleared up, wrapped in newspaper and put in the dustbin.

Henry saw that the Bee had come back and was sitting on the frame

73

of the open window, watching. 'Just wanted to make sure you were all right,' it called out to Henry.

'I'm fine, thanks,' said Henry.

Polly caught sight of the Bee and shrieked. 'There it is, Mummy! By the window. There's the nasty wasp again!'

The Mother straightened up and looked, and said, 'It's not a wasp, it's a bumblebee. You really must learn the difference, girls. Bees don't hurt you if you just leave them alone. Let's put these things away and I'll get out the Nature book and show you pictures, so you'll know another time. Bees do a lot of good, pollinating plants and so on, and I don't want you ever to harm one.'

'That's what I like to hear!' the Bee said. 'You were right about your human, after all.'

'Didn't I tell you so?' said Henry.

'Nice to know there's one garden I can visit without being whacked,' said the Bee. 'Well, so long!' And it waved cheerily to Henry and flew off.

Henry was glad to see it safely out of the way. Now there was only his own future to worry about.

The Mother put away the dustpan and brush and ushered the girls out of the room. Henry thought she had forgotten about him again, and as she passed him, he shouted to her as loudly as possible, 'Here! I'm here! Don't leave me! Put me away properly!' And he quivered with urgency.

Perhaps she heard something without realising it, or perhaps she caught sight of his stripes out of the corner of her eye. He almost swooned with delight as she reached out and picked him up, brushed him smooth with her fingers, and opened the drawer to put him inside. 'You've turned out to be a really useful bag,' she said. 'I'm glad I kept you.'

Well, Henry thought in the moment when he was flying through the air, back to his cosy drawer, *that was an adventure all right!*

He had saved the Bee, he had saved the girls from cutting themselves on the broken glass, and in the process he had got himself saved as well.

Three rescues in one day! he thought. *That's pretty good going, even for a smart fellow like me!*

And he could hardly wait for the drawer to close over him, so that he could start telling his story to the others.

Rita and the Duck

Henry had been in the dresser drawer a long time before he heard Rita's story. Rita was a strong, white bag with the word MALLARD'S printed across her front in bold black letters. Mallard's was the name of the hardware shop from which she had originally come, carrying a big bottle of liquid floor polish. Despite being so strong and useful-looking, she never seemed to want to go out, and hid herself at the bottom whenever the drawer opened, so as not to be noticed.

Once when Henry asked her if she wouldn't like to have an adventure, she said, 'No, thank you. I've had all the adventures *I* want. I'm happy staying quietly here at home.' He asked her what her adventures had been, but she wouldn't tell him. She was a paper bag who liked to keep herself to herself.

However, one rather dull day he asked her again, and with a bit of coaxing managed at last to get her to talk, just to him, quietly at the bottom of the drawer.

She had not come to Honeysuckle Cottage straight from the hardware shop, for it was not the Mother who had bought the floor polish from Mallard's that day. It was a different human altogether, who lived in a house at the other end of the village. This human had saved Rita and put her away in a drawer, until the day came when she had been brought out and filled with bread crusts. Her human was taking her little boy Toby to the countryside park to feed the ducks, and Rita was to carry the bread for them.

To begin with, Rita was quite excited to be going out. 'I was young then. I didn't know about the world, and I was restless for change,' she told Henry.

It was a bright, spring day, and the air was cool and smelled of growing things. Grey clouds were whisking across the sky, but the new grass was pushing through dark, damp earth, new leaves were unfurling, and birds everywhere were nesting. The countryside park was a wide area of woodland, with paths twisting through it, all leading to a large lake where there were lots of waterfowl – ducks and swans and geese. Children loved to come down and feed them, and the birds knew it. As soon as anyone appeared holding a paper bag, it was a signal for all of them to come swimming and waddling as fast as they could to fight for their share of the treat.

Toby's mother got Rita out of her shopping bag and gave her to Toby. He reached in for a crust of bread and started to break it up into smaller pieces. The first of the ducks arrived and clustered round his feet, quacking and nattering excitedly. They snatched up every crumb he dropped, and watched his hands to see which way he would throw the next bit. Toby was enjoying himself, laughing at the funny noises the ducks made. He tried to make sure that all of them got something. He didn't want it all to be taken by the strongest and greediest, who shoved their way to the front, and sometimes pecked the others hard to keep them away.

'Aren't they a pretty colour, Toby?' said his mother. 'Did you know they are mallard ducks? That's the same word as the one on your bread bag. Isn't that interesting?'

Toby was too excited by the ducks to pay much attention, but Rita was very interested. She hadn't realised that the word printed across her had a meaning, except for being the name of the shop. So she was named after a duck, was she? She felt rather important. Rita Mallard. None of the other bags had a surname as well as a Christian name! She couldn't wait to get home and tell them about it.

Half the bread had gone by the time the swans arrived. They had had to come from the other side of the lake. They came up paddling strongly with their great, black webs under the water. They heaved themselves out and came walking up the bank towards Toby, looking very large beside the ducks. Their big webbed feet slapped down on the path, and as they drew nearer the leading swan crooked up his neck, lowered his head and hissed at the ducks who were in his way.

Toby's mother hadn't noticed them, for she had met a friend and was chatting to her with her back turned. Toby hadn't noticed, for he had got rather a large piece of bread out, and was struggling to hold on to Rita and break up the bread at the same time.

But Rita noticed, and was alarmed. She saw how big the swans were, almost taller than Toby, and she heard the menacing things they were saying to the ducks.

'Out of the way, you lot! Come on, come on, don't you know by now all bread belongs to us? We're the kings of the lake. Shove off, or I'll peck your tail right off!'

The ducks backed away, and the swans came on. The leading one came right up to Toby and shot out its head, snatching half the bread out of Toby's hand with its big yellow beak, and nipping his fingers slightly in the process.

Toby was so surprised he gave a yell, and pulled his hands away. But that only made the swan snap even more.

'For Pete's sake, hold the bread still, kid!' the swan said crossly – though Toby, of course, couldn't understand it. He only thought it was hissing at him.

The other swans were crowding up, too, and Toby's mother looked round at last and saw what was happening. 'Look out!' she said, and started towards him.

And Toby, frightened now, dropped Rita, and ran to his mother.

'Hey!' Rita shouted in alarm. 'Don't leave me! Pick me up! Help!'

The swans were fighting with each other for the rest of the bread. It had not spilled out when she fell, and the big, hard beaks were poking and prodding and snapping, trying to get what was inside her.

'Ouch! Watch it!' she shouted at the swans. 'Leave me alone!'

They paid her no attention. They were hissing at each other and making awful threats. Finally the first swan, who was the fiercest and bossiest, grabbed Rita in his beak and, opening his wings to make himself look bigger, half waddled, half ran away. The rest followed him.

Where the lake curved, the path stopped and there was a thin edging of trees with grass and undergrowth beneath them. Here the chasing swans caught up with the leader, and there was a hissing and flapping argument, with many threats and much bad language. In the course of it Rita was dropped. She fell into the undergrowth, and not liking the idea of those beaks at all, she took the chance to wriggle further in and hide herself behind the long grass and dock leaves.

At last the row ended, with the big swan driving the others away.

'That'll show you lot who's boss around here,' he shouted as they retreated. He gave his feathers a quick tidy up, then waddled back to the water, having entirely forgotten what the argument was about.

Rita was very glad to see the back of him and his friends. But now she had another problem. Here she was, lying in the undergrowth, and her humans had no idea where she was. She could see the mother at a distance, comforting Toby, who was crying. Rita started to wriggle herself out into the open, but it was too late. The mother took Toby's hand and they walked away, continuing round the lake, getting further from Rita all the time. They had evidently forgotten all about her, or assumed she was lost for good.

Now what do I do? Rita wondered anxiously. It was the worst nightmare for a paper bag, to be left lying about in the open air. Either one got swept up and put in the rubbish bin, or caught in the rain so that one grew soggy and eventually melted away. She wanted to go home to her nice, safe drawer, but she didn't see any way of getting there now.

After a while her unhappy thoughts were disturbed by the arrival of a duck. This was a female mallard, plainer and browner than the flashy males, though with a very smart purple bar on each wing. She came pottering up, muttering to herself under her breath, evidently searching for food. Finding Rita, she said, 'I say, here's a piece of luck!' and bent her head and shoved her beak inside.

'Hey!' said Rita. 'Watch it! What do you think you're doing?'

The Duck was startled. 'Who said that? Oh, it was you, was it?'

'You can't just go shoving your beak into people without so much as a by your leave,' Rita said.

'Oh, well, I'm sorry,' the Duck said, 'but I didn't know there was a rule about it. I'm very hungry, and I've got a lot on my mind.'

'So have I,' said Rita, 'and I bet my troubles are worse than yours.'

'I bet they're not,' said the Duck. 'What's your name, by the way?'

'Rita,' said Rita, and then she remembered her surname. 'It's Rita Mallard, actually.'

'Really?' said the Duck. 'That's a coincidence. My name's Mallard, too. Helen Mallard. I wonder if we're related?'

The Duck and the paper bag looked at each other, trying to find some point of similarity. 'Maybe distant cousins,' said Rita at last, and the Duck seemed to agree.

'Well, you tell me your troubles and I'll tell you mine,' she said, 'and we'll see whose are worse.'

So Rita told her story.

'Well, that's bad, I grant you,' said Helen. 'But now listen to mine! My husband's disappeared, and I don't know where he is. He might have run off with another duck, or he might have got killed. Either way, I've got five eggs that need looking after all the time. Without him to take turns with me, I can't get off the nest to go looking for food. If I leave the eggs for too long they'll get cold and die, or else something will come along and eat them. I can't tell you how many enemies we have: foxes, stoats, weasels – even hedgehogs will take an egg. And the birds! Crows, magpies, and those dratted seagulls that hang around here all the time. Why can't they go and live by the sea like they're supposed to? Anyway, I stay as long as I can, and then dash out and try to find some food quickly. But it's not easy. So when I saw you, I was looking at the first square meal I've had in days.'

'Well,' said Rita, 'now I've heard them, I think your troubles *are* worse than mine.'

'That's nice of you,' said Helen grudgingly, 'but it doesn't really help, does it?' Anyway, I've got to get back to my eggs. I've been away too long already. Can I have the bread now?'

Rita thought quickly. 'Take me with you. Then you can eat while you're sitting on the nest.'

Helen put her head on one side. 'I suppose that's not a bad idea,' she said. 'You don't mind if I grab you and hurry? I dread to think what's happening at home.'

'Not at all,' said Rita. She thought the Duck's nest might give her more shelter if it did start to rain; and anyway, she would prefer some friendly company. Paper bags don't like being alone.

The journey to Helen's nest was uncomfortable and rather alarming, for Rita was a large bag and Helen had difficulty holding her clear of the ground, so she got rather bumped. Then suddenly Helen flung herself into the water and started paddling away from the shore.

'Don't get me wet!' Rita cried in alarm. 'It's fatal to bags.'

'Sorry,' said Helen, rather muffled. 'I'm doing my best.'

They reached the nest at last. A tree on the bank had fallen over and was lying out across the water, and Helen's nest was built on top of a pile of dead wood that had floated up against the branches and got caught.

'What a good place for a home. You're pretty snug here,' Rita said, as Helen climbed up on to the nest and put her down.

'Oh, it's not bad. It's better than the place we nested last year. That was on the shore back there, and we didn't manage to raise a single egg. Every one got taken.'

'I should think being out on the water will keep away your enemies,' said Rita.

'Well, they can still climb out along the tree trunk,' said Helen. 'I've been lucky so far, but nowhere's completely safe.' She began to settle herself fussily, pushing the eggs this way and that with her beak to get them in the right position. 'Thank heaven they're all right this time, anyway,' she said, giving a final fidget of her wings. 'Now, how about that bread?'

The Duck ate hungrily, searching Rita's corners very thoroughly for every last crumb, though she did try to be careful with her beak now she knew Rita was sensitive.

'That's better,' she said with a satisfied sigh. 'I think I'll settle down for the night. It's getting too late to go out again. Night's the worst time for enemies. And I think it's going to rain.' She eyed Rita sideways. 'So, do you want to stay the night? I suppose I *could* take you back to the shore,' she said, making it clear she didn't want to.

'Thanks, I'll stay, if you don't mind,' said Rita. 'But does it get very wet here, when it rains?'

'Oh, I forgot you were afraid of water. No, it's quite dry. The tree keeps the rain off very nicely.'

And so, indeed, Rita found that it did. When the tree had fallen, some of its roots had remained in the earth, so it was not dead but covered in leaves. Helen's nest was right in under the branches, and the leaves were thick enough to keep the nest dry and snug. Even though it rained for most of the night, Rita managed to stay dry; and lying near the Duck, it was nice and warm, too.

It was not a quiet night though, for it was very dark and all around there were strange little rustling noises that made Rita remember what Helen had said about 'the enemies'. She hardly slept a wink, wondering if every little sound meant some creature with sharp teeth was creeping towards them along the tree trunk. Helen seemed to manage to sleep all right, with her beak buried deep in the feathers of her back. Though she woke once or twice to look around her, she had no trouble in dropping off again. When the first grey light of dawn stole across the misty water, and a blackbird somewhere starting singing that the sun was on its way, Rita managed to fall asleep at last.

She was woken by Helen standing up and stretching, shaking her wings vigorously and snapping her beak a few times.

'Well, I suppose I'd better go off and get some breakfast,' she said. 'I'm absolutely starving again. You don't know how lucky you are, not having to eat.' She eyed Rita curiously. 'What do you want to do? Do you want me to take you back to the shore?'

Then Rita had her wonderful idea.

'I could stay here and egg-sit for you while you go and find food,' she said. 'I'll spread myself over them and keep them warm – paper is a wonderful insulator, you know. And if any enemies come, the eggs will be hidden.'

Helen looked pleased. 'I say, that is nice of you.'

'That's all right,' said Rita. 'We are cousins, after all. As you say, I don't need to eat, so you won't have to hurry back.'

So began Rita's new job as an egg-sitter. She laid herself over the eggs and folded her edges round them snugly, while Helen went off looking for food. It took quite a long time each day for a duck to eat enough waterweed to satisfy hunger, so she was very glad of Rita's help.  And when she was on the nest herself, she and Rita enjoyed each other's company. They chatted for hours, telling each other everything about their lives.

Rita was nervous at first, being left alone. She especially disliked the seagulls, who circled overhead making a terrible racket. Mostly what they yelled at each other was about food, and Rita was always afraid that that meant the nest she was guarding. But in fact the tree branches hid the nest completely from above, so the gulls didn't know it was there.

When trouble came it was from the direction of the shore, and it came hopping out along the tree trunk in the form of a magpie. Helen was out feeding and Rita was covering the eggs. Through the curtain of leaves she saw the magpie coming. She shuddered and tucked herself more closely round the eggs. Helen had told her that magpies were one of the worst of the enemies, who would take eggs and little chicks too. And there was nothing a duck could do about it. A magpie's beak was long and wickedly sharp. A duck's rounded beak was made for gathering weed, not for fighting.

Rita could not take her eyes from that beak as the magpie hopped cautiously along the trunk on his strong, springy legs. He was big and bold and handsome in his smart black and white, and there was a glossy green sheen to the long feathers of his tail. His eyes were bright and cunning, but, oh, most of all there was that long, black, pointed beak, hard as steel. It could tear a paper bag to shreds in a minute.

Now the shining eyes had seen her. The magpie leaned closer. The only hope, Rita thought, was to bamboozle the bird. Screwing up her courage, she said suddenly and loudly, 'Don't you know this is private property?'

The bird was startled and jumped a step backwards. It stared hard at what it could see of Rita through the fringe of leaves. 'Blimey, a talking bag! Whatever next?' it muttered to itself.

'Would you leave, please,' said Rita, trying to sound firm. 'I don't care to be stared at in my own house by strangers.'

'*Your* house?' said the Magpie in its hard, hoarse voice. 'Since when? I thought there was a duck's nest in there.'

'Whatever made you think that?' said Rita nervously.

'A fox told me,' said the Magpie. 'He caught the drake on the shore and ate it, but he didn't fancy coming out along the trunk for the Duck and the eggs. Didn't think it would take his weight, and he's not fond of the water. So what's going on?'

'The Duck left when she lost her husband,' said Rita. 'This is my home now.' The Magpie didn't seem to want to leave, and kept peering at her through the leaves, first with one eye and then the other. 'And you're trespassing,' she said.

'There's no trespass in it, when a bloke's hungry,' said the Magpie.

'Well there's nothing for you here,' said Rita.

'What happened to the eggs, then?' said the Magpie suspiciously.

'There never were any,' said Rita. 'Your friend the fox killed the drake before the Duck had started laying. He was playing a trick on you, telling you to come out here.'

'You what?' said the Magpie.

'Probably wanted to see you fall in the water,' said Rita. 'He was making a fool of you.'

'So that was his game! I wondered why he was being so helpful,' the Magpie said angrily. 'No eggs, you say?'

'Never were any,' said Rita.

'Cor! I'll give that fox what for when I see him,' said the Magpie grimly. 'Um – look, lady, sorry I disturbed you.'

'That's all right. But please leave now. I have rather a headache,' said Rita grandly, and the Magpie bowed and backed away, muttering threats towards foxes under its breath.

When she was left alone, Rita found herself trembling. She had been very frightened. But she had saved the eggs, and was rather looking forward to telling the Duck all about it. Still, she'd be glad not to have another encounter like that one.

Fortunately, there were no more bad scares, and two days later the eggs hatched. Out came five little yellow ducklings, each with a soft brown stripe down its back. Helen was delighted. 'It's thanks to you they survived,' she told Rita.

Rita was amazed to see how, almost as soon as they were out of the shell, the ducklings were ready to take to the water. 'They're hungry,' said Helen. 'I have to teach them how to eat weed. They'll be out with me all day now, so I won't need you to guard the nest. Would you like me to take you back to the shore?'

'I suppose I'd better go,' said Rita, feeling rather forlorn. 'But I don't know how I'm going to get back into a human's house. There's no life for me out in the open in the park.'

Helen thought, as well as she could with five hungry ducklings all talking to her at once. 'There are always lots of pushchairs,' she said at last. 'Suppose we could get you into one? Then they'd take you home with them without knowing.'

'Good idea. I think that's the best chance,' said Rita.

'Come on, then,' said Helen. With the ducklings swimming madly

88

behind her, Helen carried Rita back to the shore, and from a safe place in the undergrowth, they looked out for a suitable pushchair. At last a mother came by with a big double pushchair, which had a luggage space underneath the seats. Her two children were walking ahead, holding bags of bread, looking for ducks to feed. They all stopped just beyond Helen and Rita's hiding place.

As soon as they saw the mother put on the pushchair's brake, Rita said, 'That's the one! But you'll need to be quick.'

'OK,' said Helen. She turned to the ducklings. 'You children stay here. Don't move, do you hear me? I shan't be a minute.' And she waddled quickly out, across the path, and pushed Rita into the luggage rack. 'I hope you make it,' she said.

'Thanks,' said Rita. 'I shall miss you.'

'I'll miss you too – cousin,' said Helen. 'I must get back to the kids.'

'I know. Good luck with them,' said Rita.

She felt sad as she watched Helen hurrying away, back into the shadow of the trees where her family waited. She had enjoyed their friendship and their talks. And her own future was very uncertain. Even if she was taken to a human home, there was no knowing what would happen to her afterwards.

But of course, it was Polly's and Betty's pushchair she had hitched a ride on, and their Mother was very good and careful with paper bags. Rita was found when the Mother got home, was smoothed out and put into the drawer.

'And I've been here ever since,' said Rita to Henry. 'So you can see now why I don't want any more adventures. I make sure I keep down

89

at the bottom whenever the drawer opens. And if you'd ever had to face a hungry magpie you'd do the same.'

'You may be right,' said Henry.

Rita sighed a little. 'But I do often wonder what happened to the ducklings. We were related, after all. And I was a sort of second mother to them.'

The Cheese Sandwiches Find a Home

When Verso and Recto heard Henry shout, 'Now! Run!' they didn't hesitate. They flung themselves off the paper plate and began running down the hill towards the trees as fast as they could. They knew they were running for their lives, and fear gave them wings. At any moment, they thought they would hear a human voice giving the alarm, the thump of human feet chasing them, feel human hands grabbing them. After that, it would be the teeth! It didn't bear thinking about. So they ran until they nearly burst.

It was hard getting through the long grass. It was like a jungle to them, with the meadowsweet, ragwort and knapweed towering up like tall trees. Little creatures hopped and wriggled away as they ran, scurrying ants and scuttling beetles, centipedes a moving ripple of feet. Tiny moths flew up in a panic crying, 'Oh dear! Oh dear!' Crickets bounced as though they were on springs. A spider dropped suddenly down to the end of his thread and goggled at them. 'Who goes there?' he demanded, but they rushed past him.

There was such a whispering and murmuring of comment on their passing—

'Who are they?'

'What's wrong?'

'There they go!'

—that they were afraid the humans must hear it. But to human ears it would have sounded only like the wind in the grass; even when a wriggling knot of cinnabar caterpillars, like a tangle of striped socks, raised their heads from munching on a ragwort plant and positively yelled, 'Look out! Monsters! Catch 'em!'

At last the grass thinned out and grew shorter, and then there were patches of moss and bare earth which were easier underfoot, and then at last they had reached the wood. They dashed in among the trees and got behind the first big trunk, and for a moment all they could do was to lean against it, panting, listening for sounds of pursuit.

But all was quiet, except for the wind fooling about in the leaves up above them. At last Verso said, 'I don't think they saw us. Have a look.'

Recto cautiously peered out round the tree trunk. He could see the humans up at the top of the slope. They seemed to have caught Henry, and were going back to their picnic. There were no sounds of alarm. No one was coming after them.

'We've done it,' Recto said. 'We're safe.'

'Good old Henry,' said Verso. 'He's saved us.'

'I wish we could thank him,' Recto said. 'He'll never know we got safely away.'

'Oh, I expect he could see us when he was up in the air,' said Verso. 'He'll know we're all right.'

'Well, what do we do now?' said Recto.

'We'd better go further into the wood,' said Verso. 'Just in case anyone comes after us. And then we'd better find ourselves somewhere to sleep.'

The wood seemed enormous and dark and frightening. There were strange smells and strange cries, little rustling noises in the undergrowth, and the sense of many eyes watching them. Verso and Recto hurried along, staring about nervously, without any idea where they were going or what they would find when they got there.

It seemed to be getting darker and, equally worried about night falling or rain starting, they looked about them for somewhere to shelter. They came upon a tree that had a triangular hole at the base of the trunk, and thought it would make a good hiding place. They stepped inside, and found it dry, with a comfortable carpet of dead leaves underfoot. Wearily but gratefully, they sat down.

'This is quite nice,' Verso said, trying to look on the bright side. 'It's dry and warm. Perhaps we could make it our home.'

'Well, perhaps,' said Recto. He was glad enough to stop for a while, anyway. He leaned back wearily, only to straighten up with a startled yelp.

'What is it?' asked Verso anxiously.

'Something sharp,' he said, feeling behind him carefully. 'A lot of sharp somethings, like bristles. And they're moving!' To his horror, he found the bristly thing seemed to be growing bigger. They had to dash for the entrance hole or they'd have been squashed and impaled. Outside they stood, staring into the dark hole with a mixture of fear and curiosity. There was something brown and prickly in there which had been curled up in a tight ball and was now uncurling, filling the space inside. Soon there appeared a long snout and two little dark eyes, and a rather cross individual came grumbling out.

'Hmph! Huh! Botheration! Can't a person sleep in his own house without being sat on?' he muttered. He stared from one to another and said, 'What on earth are you?'

'We're cheese sandwiches,' said Verso. 'And we didn't know it was your house. We're sorry for disturbing you.'

'What are you?' Recto asked.

'I'm a hedgehog, of course,' said the creature. 'I've lived here all my life, and I've never seen anything like *you* in the wood.'

'We're escaping from a terrible fate and trying to make our way in the world,' said Recto. 'What we mostly need now is somewhere safe to stay.'

94

'Well, you can't stay in my house,' the Hedgehog said. But it was sniffing at them, its long, flexible nose twitching. 'Although – I must say, you smell rather nice. Almost as if you'd be good to eat.'

Recto's bread turned pale. 'Oh no,' he said quickly, 'hedgehogs can't eat cheese sandwiches. Instant death. Absolute poison to your sort, honestly.'

'How do you know?' the Hedgehog said suspiciously. 'A minute ago you didn't even know what a hedgehog was.'

'I – um – I remember reading about it,' said Recto, inventing wildly. 'In a book. It said particularly that hedgehogs must never, ever eat cheese sandwiches. They must stick to – er—'

'Their usual – er—' Verso tried to help. 'What do you usually eat?'

'Beetles and worms, mostly,' said the Hedgehog. 'Slugs. That sort of thing. Is that what it said in the book?'

'Absolutely,' said Verso.

'Definitely,' said Recto. 'Especially the worms.'

'Oh,' said the Hedgehog. 'Well, in that case, I'd better give you a miss. Though you do smell rather interesting.'

95

'Well, sorry again to have disturbed you,' Verso said, backing off, tugging at Recto urgently.

'Oh – er – yes, we must be off,' said Recto. 'Be getting dark soon. Cheerio, then.'

And they hurried away, not daring to look back. They were following a faint path which wound about through the trees, and after a while they came round a corner to find another creature in front of them, busily digging a hole. It was very attractive-looking, with thick grey-brown fur and a long, beautiful tail like a fountain of silver. Verso felt sure no one as beautiful as that could be dangerous to them. They stopped where they were, and the creature looked over its shoulder, saw them, and at once set up a scream of annoyance.

'No looking! No looking! I know what you're after! Turn away at once!'

'Sorry, sorry,' said Recto. 'We didn't mean to look.'

'It's very rude to watch a squirrel bury his nuts,' said the creature angrily. 'Don't you know *anything*?'

'Sorry, we're new here,' said Verso. 'We won't look, honestly.'

They turned away and listened to the scrabbling and scratching sounds, until after a moment the Squirrel said, rather more calmly, 'All right, you can look now.'

They turned back. It seemed pleased with itself, stroking its whiskers and flirting its lovely tail. 'Well?' it demanded. 'Can you tell?'

'Tell what?' said Verso.

'Where it is, of course. Where I was digging. Can you see anything? I bet you can't.'

Recto was wise enough to say, 'No, I can't see anything at all,' and to sound admiring while he was about it.

'How very clever you must be,' said Verso, picking up the cue.

'Oh well,' said the Squirrel casually, 'I've been about it some time now. Buried hundreds of nuts in this wood. *Hundreds*. None of them has ever been found. I don't like to boast, but I must be one of the top nut bury-ers in this wood. But what are you?'

'We're cheese sandwiches, and we're escaping from a terrible fate and trying to make our way in the world,' said Recto.

'Sandwiches, eh?' said the Squirrel, suddenly interested. Its whiskers twitched as it tried to smell them. 'I've heard of sandwiches. They're a human thing – made of bread. I like bread. I had some once. A human dropped some up near the car park.'

'Oh no, we're not that sort of sandwich,' said Recto hastily. 'Not at all. That's something quite different.'

'You *smell* like bread,' the Squirrel said, sniffing.

'Well, we're not. And by the way,' said Verso, in a firm but kindly tone, 'I ought to tell you that it's considered very rude where we come from to sniff at people.'

'Oh, sorry,' said the Squirrel, taken aback. 'I never heard of any rules about smelling. Actually, I do it all the time.'

'We didn't know about your not-looking rule,' said Verso kindly.

'Takes all sorts, I suppose,' said the Squirrel. 'I must get on. Got a lot of dashing about to do.' He started to turn away, then stopped. 'Did you want something, by the way?'

'We're looking for a safe place to stay,' said Recto.

'Get high up, that's my advice,' said the Squirrel. 'My dray's at the

97

top of the highest tree in the wood, out of the way of all the nasty things that creep up on you at night – foxes and stoats and that sort of cattle. Get up high and keep out of the way, that's the best thing. Only way to get a good night's sleep.'

'Thanks,' said Verso. 'We'll remember that. Well, cheerio.'

'Bye,' said the Squirrel, and dashed off with a flick of his tail and disappeared.

Verso and Recto walked on. 'Can we possibly get up high?' Verso asked. 'It sounds like a good idea.'

'I'm not sure I could climb a tree. And what if we met another squirrel?' said Recto. 'Sooner or later they'd decide we were made of bread and take a bite out of us.'

'They could do that on the ground just as well,' said Verso. 'I'm for trying the tree idea.'

'What tree idea is that?' said a very small voice from somewhere nearby. The sandwiches looked about, startled, and at first could not see anyone. And then they saw it – a tiny brown mouse with a very long tail, almost hidden under a large dock leaf. It was holding a small blackberry in its paws, but the blackberry was very unripe – almost completely green.

'Oh, hullo!' said Verso. 'We didn't see you there. What are you up to?'

'Same as every creature in the wood, I should think – looking for food,' said the Mouse. It threw away the berry with a look of bitterness. 'Hard as a stone. And it tastes nasty.'

'It's not ripe,' said Recto.

'Well, I *know* that,' said the Mouse. 'It's a bad time of year, this –

98

flowers gone and berries not ready. I don't know what an honest chap is supposed to do. And what are you two up to, if it comes to that? You're strange-looking mice, I must say.'

'Oh, we're not mice,' said Recto. 'We're—'

Verso hadn't liked all the talk about food, and she kicked Recto to shut him up and said, 'We're travellers, just passing through. We're escaping from a terrible fate and trying to make our way in the world.'

The Mouse was interested. 'Oh, really? What sort of terrible fate?'

'We don't like to talk about it,' said Verso quickly. 'The thing is, we need somewhere safe to sleep for the night, and we were thinking of trying up in the trees. A squirrel said that was a good place.'

'Squirrels!' said the Mouse. 'What do they know? Big thugs, always getting to the nuts first and hogging the lot!'

'Well, we were rather put off by his rough ways ourselves,' said Verso. 'But he mentioned lots of nasty things that live on the ground so we though maybe it would be safer up in a tree.'

The Mouse regarded them sideways with its bright little eye, its nose and whiskers working away all the time. 'Didn't mention the other bad things in the trees, I suppose?'

'Er – not really,' said Recto.

'The birds? Worse than the squirrels, if anything. They come down in flocks and eat all the berries before the rest of us get a look in. *And* anything else they can get their beaks on. And where do they live? Up in the trees.'

'Oh,' said Recto. 'Perhaps it's not as nice up there as he made it sound.'

'No, you don't want to be climbing trees. A nice cosy hole in the ground, that's what you need. I'd invite you home with me, but you'd never fit into my place – especially as the wife's just had another litter.'

'Oh, congratulations,' said Verso. 'How nice for you.'

'Ten she had this time,' said the Mouse. 'Ten new mouths to feed, and at this time of year! However,' he went on, recollecting himself, 'I do know of a nice hole, very close to mine, that might do. It was started by a rabbit, but he gave it up after a couple of hours' digging and went somewhere else. That's rabbits for you – always starting things and not finishing them. Scatterbrained, the lot of them.' He sniffed disapprovingly. 'Anyway, the hole's there, and it's empty. I'd be happy to show you the way if you like.'

The Mouse hadn't said anything about eating them, and seemed too small to be dangerous, so Recto said, 'Thanks, that's nice of you. Is it far?'

'No, not far. We'd be neighbours – I could tell you a lot of useful stuff about the wood, since you don't seem to know anything.' He looked sidelong at them again, smirking under his whiskers.

He scuttled off, keeping to the cover of the grass and weeds, and the sandwiches followed as well as they could, tripping on grass roots and bumping into dandelions. The Mouse paused every now and then to let them catch up, then scurried on again. Finally they came to a place where the ground had sunk a little, leaving the higher ground like a sort of bank. Trees growing on the bank had had their roots exposed, and there were a number of interesting hollows and holes among them.

'Mine's up there,' said the Mouse, gesturing higher up and further along. 'Won't take you there now, don't want to disturb the missus. But the hole I was talking about is here.'

It was not much more than a shallow cave, scraped out behind a large root, but it was dry and clean and just big enough for Verso and Recto to get in and turn round. Best of all, when they were inside, the tree root hid the hole from sight, unless any creature should come right up to it. It seemed the best they could hope for.

'It's very nice,' said Recto.

'I thought you'd like it,' said the Mouse, looking pleased with himself. 'Now, why don't you settle in here, while I pop off home. I'll come back later and see how you're getting on.'

'Thank you. You're very kind,' said Recto.

'Might bring a few of my friends to see you,' the Mouse said. 'Friends and family. They'd be interested to meet you, I'm sure.'

'Oh, well, do,' said Verso. 'Though we haven't got anything to offer, in the way of refreshments.'

'Just yourselves will do very well,' said the Mouse with a wink, and disappeared into the grass.

'What a nice chap,' said Recto. 'I think we'll do all right here, don't you? It's as good as anything we're likely to find, and it's nice to have friendly neighbours.'

'I suppose so,' said Verso. 'This place isn't very big, though. I mean, I can't see it as a permanent home.'

'Well, maybe some of the neighbours will dig it out for us, make it bigger. These little creatures are great diggers, you know, and they do seem friendly.'

There was a very small sniggering sound at that point, and a rustling movement in the dead leaves in front of the hole.

'Who's there?' Recto said sharply. 'Come on, show yourself! Don't hide there like a coward, laughing, or I'll . . .'

The leaves parted and a worm stuck its head out. 'Or you'll what?' it demanded. 'Boy oh boy, you're green, the pair of you! I heard it all – all that stuff from the Mouse about settling in, and you twittering about good neighbours. Oh, it's rich, that is!' And the Worm sniggered again, making the leaves shake with its laughter.

'I don't see what's so funny,' said Recto. 'We needed a shelter and the Mouse found us one.'

'Yes, nice and handy for his own hole,' said the Worm. 'So that he and his wife and kids and all their friends can pop round and eat you. Didn't mention that bit, did he?'

'Eat us?' said Verso, horrified. 'But he never said anything about eating us.'

'Course he didn't. He's not stupid. You'd have legged it if he had. Now he's got you tucked up safe and sound in his own larder.'

'Please don't say that word,' said Recto with a shudder. 'Look, I'm not sure the Mouse had any idea what we are. We didn't tell him, and he never asked.'

'Got a nose, hasn't he? Same as anyone else. Bread and cheese – a mouse's favourite nosh, *if* he can get hold of 'em. Why you'd accept help from someone who wants to eat you I'll never understand, but it's got its funny side.' And it sniggered again.

'We didn't know,' said Verso. 'We thought he was being nice.'

'Anyway, how to we know *you* don't want to eat us?' said Recto

'Do me a favour,' said the Worm. 'I'm a vegan. Plant matter only. I'm very particular what I eat, and it doesn't include the likes of you. Look here, if I was you I'd leg it as fast as I could, before that lot get back. You wouldn't stand a chance if the whole tribe comes.'

'But where can we go?' Recto asked wearily. 'It seems to me that everyone wants to eat us. How can we keep ourselves safe?'

'Well,' said the Worm thoughtfully, 'there is one place I can think of. I've never been there myself, but I've heard of it. It's a human place, and it's fenced all round, and the ground is concreted over – that's why I've never been there. I like to travel underground, you see. But the concrete and the fencing mean there are no foxes, stoats, weasels, rats and the like.'

'But there'd be humans,' said Verso. 'You said it was a human place.'

'Yes, but they only go there in the daytime, and there's plenty of places to hide. Once the place closes, you'd have it to yourselves.'

'What is it, exactly?' asked Recto.

'It's a model village. All laid out like a human town, but tiny. They've got everything there, so I hear – houses, shops, a castle, schools, hotels, docks, a fairground, a boating lake – oh, everything! And there's a model railway with little trains that run all round it. Now, it seems to me,' said the Worm, 'that you could pick yourself a nice house to hide in during the day, while the humans are there. They're only allowed in at certain times, so they wouldn't be able to creep up on you. And they have to keep to the paths and aren't allowed to touch anything. You'd be safe inside, not just from humans but from anything that did manage to get in – birds, for instance, or squirrels. Then when the place shuts, you could enjoy yourselves. Ride about in the trains, go on the boats, anything you liked.'

'It sounds wonderful,' Verso said. 'But how would we get there?'

'Oh, it isn't far from here. I can tell you the first bit of the way, and after that you'll have to follow the signs. But you'd better get moving. That mousey lot'll be coming back any time.'

'All right, we'll do it,' said Recto. 'What's this place called?'

'The model village? It's called Beaconscot,' said the Worm. 'OK, this is the way you go from here . . .'

It was a long and hard journey, harder than they had expected, and they had enough adventures on the way to have kept a paper bag talking for a year. The last part was the worst, when they had to move along human streets and keep themselves hidden from human eyes. It took them two days, and at times they almost gave up in despair, but at last they came to the entrance, with the arched sign over the gate: Beaconscot. They lay up behind some broken flowerpots near the entrance until it was almost closing time and most people had gone away. Then they slipped in and hid again, behind the ticket hut, where there was a pile of wood. When everyone had gone, the gates were locked and everything was quiet, they came out and made their way down the tarmac path to the model village itself.

It was more like a town than a village. The worm had been right – there was *everything* there, including a lot of little plaster people and animals doing human things, like waiting for buses and visiting the zoo and playing cricket. There were even some plaster people having a picnic, which made Verso and Recto shudder, remembering how it had all started.

But the place was perfect for them. Verso was so excited by the choice of houses that they moved from one to another every night for the first couple of weeks, until Recto put his foot down, and said she must choose once and for all. They settled at last in a nice Victorian villa in a quiet part of the town, but not too far from the shops and the railway station. They were perfectly happy there, hiding in their nice house by day, and coming out to explore their town by night. No one ever found them or disturbed them, and best of all, no one ever tried to eat them.

And for all I know, they are probably living there still.

Henry's Last Great Adventure

Henry lived a long and happy life in the dresser drawer, but the time came when he grew old. His paper grew soft and creased, and here and there it was worn nearly through. His fine blue stripes were faded and dull. He didn't care about going out any more. He managed to work his way underneath the other bags, so that when a human opened the drawer he was hidden from sight, and would not be disturbed. He'd had many adventures in the past, but now he just wanted peace and quiet.

He still listened to the stories the other paper bags told – for telling stories is the thing that paper bags like best in the world to do. Sometimes he grumbled that the stories weren't as good as they had been in his young days, and the adventures in them weren't a patch on his own. Bags nowadays were a namby-pamby lot, he would say, always fussing about keeping themselves clean. They weren't daring and bold as he and his friends had been. 'You don't get adventures without creases,' he would say.

106

The other bags didn't mind his grumbling. That was what old bags always did, after all! Sometimes they would try to coax him into telling one of his stories, which were famous throughout the kitchen. Sometimes Henry would oblige, and he still enjoyed the rapt attention they gave him when he told a good one. But on other days he would just mumble, 'Oh, you've got your own stories. You don't need mine.' And then no wheedling would move him. He would just wriggle to the bottom of the drawer and go to sleep.

He slept a lot now, drifting in and out of dreams. The dreams were rather like the adventures of his youth, only better, because he knew how the adventures had ended, while the dreams could go in any direction. Surprising things often happened in them. Sometimes he was a little bit grumpy when the other bags woke him up with their noise, and he would tell them off. They would pretend to be afraid of him, and then laugh among themselves.

As he slept more and more, the dreams came to seem much more real than anything else, so that it was sometimes hard for him to know whether he was really awake or asleep.

He dreamed one day (or perhaps it wasn't a dream) that the drawer had been left open. Outside, the kitchen was full of sunshine and the air smelled warm and drowsy – like late-summer afternoon with a hint of freshly-baked cakes. Henry was suddenly seized with the desire to go out, and see the big, wide world just once more. He worked his way to the top of the drawer and looked out. The kitchen window was wide open, letting in the soft golden air. He could see the sunny garden beyond it, full of flowers and the quick little movements of bees and butterflies. A line of washing was waving its arms in the gentle breeze. He could hear sparrows fooling about in the ivy that grew up the back of the house, and starlings chattering and whistling to each other. Further away in a high tree a robin was spinning out its song like a silver thread.

The breeze came wandering in at the window, played idly with the curtains and then tried to make a pencil roll off the kitchen table. Henry made an effort to heave himself up on to the lip of the drawer, and called out, 'I say! Over here!'

The Breeze drifted over. 'Hello, old timer. What do you want?'

'I was wondering if you'd mind taking me for a ride,' said Henry. 'I used to fly a lot when I was younger, but it's years since I last had a trip. I'd like to see the big, wide world just once more, from up there in the sky.'

'No problemo, Dad,' said the Breeze. 'It'll be fun. How'll we do it? You want me to get underneath you?' And he fingered the Henry's frayed edge – which had once been sharply deckled, long ago in the bookshop.

'No, lad, you might drop me,' said Henry. 'I've done this before, and the best way is for you to get right inside me.'

'Okey doke,' said the Breeze. 'Open wide, then.'

And the next moment the Breeze had whipped him out, across the kitchen and through the open window. It felt so nice after such a long time in the bottom of the drawer, that Henry felt suddenly younger. He was ready for another adventure. He laughed aloud. 'This is nice!' he said. 'Take me higher!'

'If you say so,' said the Breeze, and went climbing up the sky, pushing Henry in front of him.

The air was warm and sweet with summer. There were shimmering threads of spindrift in it, and flower seeds swinging on their silken parachutes. Henry saw damsel flies, so delicate they were almost transparent. Birds, as solid to him as aeroplanes are to us, went beating by. He looked down and saw the cottage that had been his home for so long, the green of the garden, splashed with bright colour from the dahlias. Beyond the garden there were fields, framed all round with tall hedges of hawthorn, just beginning to be painted with berries. There were black and white cows dozing in the shade, swishing their tails and flapping their ears against the flies. There were brown ponies grazing with steady, juicy crunches.

'Higher, higher!' said Henry, and the Breeze took him further up.

Now he could see the black streaks of the roads, and the movement and glitter of cars. He saw the heath, dappled with the purple of heather bloom. He saw the village, crouching in a fold of the land and people going about their daily chores.

'Higher, higher!' said Henry.

He saw the town, a great sprawl of buildings and roads and traffic, but he was too high now to hear its clamour. There was no sound at all, just the sweet movement of the air around him. The earth seemed far away. The sky seemed close and real, dense like thick blue cream.

'Look out,' said the Breeze, 'here's a cloud.'

He carried Henry up through it. Suddenly the blue was gone and all was grey-white and misty. The cloud was damp and smelled warm and clean, like the steam in the kitchen on washing day. Then he was out again and into the deep blue air above, and there was nothing to see below him but the white curdles of the cloud.

'I'm going to put you down here for a bit,' said the Breeze. 'You're heavier than you look. I need a rest.'

Henry didn't mind. He wasn't the least bit afraid, though he was a very long way from the ground. The Breeze set him down on the cloud, and he sank into it just a little, as though it were a big, white feather duvet. It was very comfortable.

'Take your time,' Henry said to the Breeze. 'I'm happy just to sit here for a bit.'

The sunshine beat down on him, but though it was clear and bright it didn't seem at all hot. There were no birds up this high, no creatures at all,  and no sound of any sort. It was so pleasant, Henry thought he might just take a little nap.

After a time he heard a voice say, 'Hello, Henry.'

He was feeling so sleepy he wasn't even startled; but when he turned his head, what he saw took his breath away. It was a carrier bag of such beauty as he could never have imagined. It was green, but a shade of green so rich and vibrant it was like the colour of every living thing on earth, distilled into the essence of life itself. Its surface seemed to ripple and shimmer with light, so that Henry felt there must be wonderful pictures to be seen in the ripples if only he could concentrate enough. It was hard to look at the Carrier because of its great beauty; and it was strangely hard to tell how big it was. Sometimes it seemed it must be as big as the whole world, and very far off; and sometimes it seemed normal-sized, close by and touchable.

Henry felt he could never have enough of gazing. Surely this must be a very great Being indeed. Shyly, he said, 'How do you know my name?'

'I know all the names of all my people,' said the deep, wonderful voice.

Then Henry knew. 'So there really is a Great Green Carrier after all,' he said. 'I thought it was only a story.'

'Many things that are stories are also true,' said the Being

'But was it really *you* that Colin saw?' Henry asked, because the Great Green Carrier in Colin's story had been so – well, so *ordinary* in comparison.

'What Colin saw was a messenger, who resembled the Great Green Carrier just a little, just enough to do his job. There are many such. I, too, am only a messenger. My Master is infinitely greater than me, and I resemble him only a little.'

'I can't imagine anyone greater than you,' said Henry.

'No one can. That's why there are messengers. But you yourself, Henry, resemble Him, just a little. All creatures are like their maker, in their own way. That is the way the world works.'

'Then, if you are not the Great Green Carrier, who are you?'

'You may call me Michael,' said the Being.

Henry thought about things for a while, and then he said, 'Is this a dream?'

Michael seemed to shimmer in a way that made him look as though he was smiling. 'Some say that all of life is a dream, and that we wake up at life's end.'

'But that isn't an answer to my question,' Henry said.

'Some questions don't have an answer,' said Michael. 'And there are many things you are not permitted to know at present, but which will become clear in time. Be patient, little bag. All will be well.'

There followed a silence, which seemed to Henry to go on for many years, during which wonderful images and thoughts flitted through his mind. The sun stood still overhead, the clouds ceased to drift and the wind ceased to blow. All was calm and quiet, and he felt a happiness so deep it seemed to fill him with a golden light.

And after this unknown length of time, Michael said, 'Pleasant as this is, Henry, you cannot stay here. It is not your time yet. You must go back. But is there anything you wish to ask me before I return you?'

'Yes, there is one thing,' Henry said, and the golden peace left him as he thought of it. He swallowed hard. 'It's about – about *recycling*.' Like many other paper bags, he didn't even like to think the word, let alone say it. But this might be his one chance to learn the truth.

'What is it you wish to know?' Michael asked.

'Well, about what it's like,' Henry said anxiously. 'You see, I'm afraid of it,' he admitted.

Michael's shimmering changed to a pattern that was loving and reassuring. 'There's no need to be afraid. Recycling comes to all of us. It is a natural process.'

'But – doesn't it hurt?' Henry asked in a small voice. 'Being made back into pulp again?'

'No, because it's only your paper that will be returned to pulp. Your spirit, the thing that makes you Henry and no one else, will have departed already.'

'But then, doesn't that mean that I'll be nothing at all any more? That I'll just be gone and lost?'

'Nothing is ever lost, and nothing is ever wasted. Remember that,' said Michael. 'You will join with the spirit of the Great One and be part of Him. That is the way of all things in our world, even human beings. But their Great One is the greatest of all.'

Henry felt comforted, and thought about these things until Michael said, 'And now I must send you back.'

Henry looked around. All was still, and the air did not move. 'The Breeze has gone,' he said. And he felt glad just for a moment, because perhaps that would mean he wouldn't have to go back after all. It was so lovely here, he'd have liked to stay for ever.

Michael seemed to know his thought. 'When you come again, it will be to stay. But for now, I will send you back on my breath.'

That part was just like Colin's story, Henry thought, when *his* Great Green Carrier had blown him off the shelf. He understood then a little of what Michael had meant, about the messenger resembling the master. He looked round to tell Michael about this idea, and discovered to his amazement that he was already far, far away from the cloud, which was almost out of sight. He had not felt a thing, but he was swinging and planing gently down towards the earth, borne on an air warmer and sweeter than any he had ever known.

Below him the earth was wide and green and blurred. Gradually as he drifted closer he began to see more details, the great mountains and lakes and cities and the roads between them. Then he could see the town nearest to his village, then the village itself and the fields around it. Then he was close enough to see the heath, his own cottage, and the garden, with the bright dahlias and the washing still blowing on the line. And then he was rushing at what seemed like great speed towards the kitchen window. He passed through it, across to the dresser, and drifted into the drawer at last quite slowly and gently, as though waking from a pleasant sleep.

Everything seemed just the same, as though he had been gone no time at all. And yet inside him everything felt different, as though he had been away for years. The singing silence of the upper sky gradually left him. The sounds of the kitchen slowly tuned in, the birdsong from outside, the sound of a fly worrying about by the window, the slip-slap of the washing machine, the murmuring voices of the other paper bags.

He looked at them, and they all seemed very young to him; but where before that had sometimes irritated him, now he felt only a warm affection for them. One of them, named Thomas, saw him smiling, and said, 'What's up, Henry? You look cheerful all of a sudden.'

114

'I've just had a wonderful adventure,' he said. 'Perhaps the best one of my life.'

'What?' said Thomas. 'But you haven't been anywhere. You've been lying there snoozing all day.'

'Oh, have I?' said Henry mysteriously. 'Then I take it you don't want to hear my new story?'

Several of the others jostled nearer, nudging Thomas urgently to keep quiet. Old Henry's stories were not to be missed, and if he had a new one, that would be really something! Life in the drawer without stories would be a desert of boredom.

'Of course we want to hear it,' they said.

'Tell us, Henry.'

'Please, please.'

'We're all listening.'

So Henry told them the story of his last, great adventure. Afterwards there was much discussion among the young bags as to whether it really had been an adventure, or only a dream; whether it was true, or just a story.

But as Michael had said to Henry, many things that are stories are also true. Henry had discovered that the division between the two was not as absolute as he had once thought. What he did know was that his last adventure was the greatest of all, and that it was only just beginning; and the wonderful story of it would never come to an end.

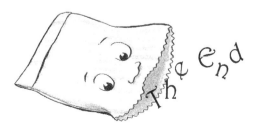

The End

Byyyyeeeeeeeeee!

Lightning Source UK Ltd.
Milton Keynes UK
UKHW050419251120
374017UK00001B/1